CHRISTOFFER V. JUNROS

Origin Andromeda

The Beginning

This novel is entirely a work of fiction. The names,
characters and incidents portrayed in it are the work
of the author's imagination. Any resemblance to
actual persons, living or dead, events or localities is
entirely coincidental.

ISBN: 978-91-527-3838-2

Editing by Dr.Jeff
Proofreading by Ann-Cristin Vuolo Junros
First edition

This book was professionally typeset on Reedsy.
Find out more at reedsy.com

This book is dedicated to my incredible wife
Joanna (Nashmil) Junros

And my always supporting mother
Ann-Cristin Vuolo Junros.

Without your support, this would never have been
possible.

Acknowledgement

Without any specific ordering and with the knowledge that this list can't include everyone, I give my highest regards and respect to *Isaac Asimov, Arthur C. Clarke, Robert Sheckley, Frank Herbert, Philip K. Dick* and many more who have written some of the most creative writings ever.

Not forgetting the respect I have for all of you who have worked with masterpieces like Stargate, Dr Who, Star Trek, Babylon 5, Star Wars, Firefly, The Matrix...I'm pausing the list here since the true length of this acknowledgment list would be too long and too boring to read.

These and many other science fiction books, series and films have shaped me and my life to this day and they continue to do so, and if you are reading this I hope that this book will shape you in one way or the other, *if only just by a little.*

Part 1, The cube!

Henrik Harlacker opens the door to their house and scratches the itchy stubble on his chin with his right hand. He is a thirty-four-year-old man with a by now at least three- or four-day-old beard stubble. He can't remember the last time he shaved but it could have been this Tuesday or maybe Wednesday. Henrik wonders if he might just let it grow into a glorious full beard. Joanna, his loving and beautiful wife, would surely love it, he believes.

Henrik and Joanna met a couple of years ago, and the moment he saw her he knew that she was the one for him. Her mesmerizing personality and timeless beauty made his heart beat faster and stronger every time he thought of her. A year later, they got married, the happiest day of their lives. The way she seamlessly owned any room she entered, becoming the centre of everyone's attention, combined with her quick mind and in-tellect, made her a naturally born leader, a figure of authority. Henrik found this very attractive and was fascinated by her.

After a long week in the office, he is glad that they are finally relaxing on the sofa together, at this moment on this Friday evening. He doesn't know that their existence will drastically change quite soon. At this moment, Henrik is just an ordinary man with an ordinary life who enjoys the small things. He is not yet aware of the dangers lurking in a very near future light-years away from his sofa.

On their comfortable sofa, they relax and enjoy a glass of red wine; there are some fresh dates and some fine chocolate on the table in front of them. The bottle was recommended by a close friend years ago on one of their vacations to the Middle East and has since then been their favourite; they always keep at least one bottle in their cellar. The living room is filled with green plants of various sizes, some smaller and some rather larger ones that have been allowed to spread out and claim their place in the room.

Along the wall hang pictures with varying motivational texts beside different animals. Together the frames form geometrical shapes. Joanna has a sharp eye for interior decoration and their home would fit perfectly into any catalogue. The windows facing the garden run from one side of the room to the other, from floor to ceiling. Along the windows,

Henrik has lowered the floor and planted palm trees together with smaller plants.

Joanna leans her head flirtatiously against Henrik as she smiles with her eyes to make him massage her tired feet. Henrik smiles back. He takes off her white socks and puts his warm hands on her cold foot as he slowly begins to massage one foot at a time while they watch the opening scene of the movie she had suggested the night before. It's an action movie starring Jason Statham, their favourite cool-guy character in any movie.

It's now Monday morning again. Henrik wakes up as usual, at 05:15. The sun's warm rays slowly find their way in through the slots between the blinds travelling up against the wall. The air in the bedroom is cool and fresh since the window was left ajar during the night. Outside, he can hear the birds chirping their morning salute together in a sweet summer symphony.

Beside him, he can hear Joanna's calm, relaxed breathing; it looks like she is dreaming about something nice.

"Perhaps you dream about waves hitting the beach, while we are flying in the sky together? Who knows?" he softly whispers to himself.

Her feminine lips form a weak smile. The slender body that barely can be seen under the thin summer blanket and her ever-so-familiar scent makes him want to stay in bed beside her, to keep dreaming through the morning in pace with her calm heart-beat, thinking, *"Only 10 more minutes."*

He reluctantly decides that he should prepare for the day, so he slowly gets out of the bed, gently closing the door when he is out of the bedroom to allow Joanna to sleep in peace. Henrik is back to work after a long weekend. He opens the door to his office, which is decorated in beautiful natural colours and filled with big green plants. Among them is a tall old fig whose top is bent downwards, just like it once had been outdoors covered with heavy snow. It is a beautiful plant that always gives him peace when needed. Built into a wall beside the fig is a relatively large aquarium where colourful Cichlids from Africa swim.

He sits on his leather chair. He shakes off the need for a refreshing cup of coffee buzzing in his brain, as he usually wants to start the computer first, allowing it to wake up during the time he finds a cup of coffee. On his large, rectangular dark wooden table, two big screens are positioned at an inwards angle; a black, ergonomically-designed keyboard with a smooth rounded shape together with a mouse that is equipped with programmable buttons complement the keyboard.

Henrik never leaves his desk untidy; he always makes sure that everything is in order before he

4

ends his day at the office. So, he was a little confused when he saw a dark cube about the size of an orange along with a note with the text *"From Viterin"* resting behind the right screen. He picks up the cube, inspects it, rotates it, feeling the perfectly shaped sides against his fingers.

Henrik slowly realizes that the cube is getting warm and a slight vibration spreads throughout his fingers. The smooth sides of the cube now pulsate in a pale blue tone and in the middle of the cube, an image begins to take shape. He is fascinated by its beauty, by its warmth. A few seconds later he can see the contours of the image taking a clearer form.

"It looks a bit like a galaxy .. maybe .. what can it be?"

A few minutes later, the image is now clear. Henrik can see the incredibly detailed image of a galaxy. He stares, wide-eyed, feeling a little tingling sensation as he is swallowed up by the picture. Then suddenly everything is black. Life is perceived as a feeling of endless space without boundaries, in addition to an unpleasant feeling of weighing a lot while simultaneously weighing nothing at all, a sense of falling combined with complete stillness at the same time, he can see a dim light in his field of view.

Terrified, he whispers, "Am I dead?"

It is black everywhere except for the galaxy that is in the middle of his view. Henrik is floating in space. He can see all the individual stars shine clearly in the smallest detail. He can feel that there is an incredibly powerful force in the middle of the galaxy, a presence that fills up all existence, it makes him feel small, tiny even. He calms himself down by focusing on a breathing technique he once learned while travelling, he realizes that he must be inside the picture now, almost in the same way as when he puts his VR headset on, but with perfect picture quality.

What is this? Immediately after the thought, a box appears to the right in his field of view, with the text:

"Messier 31,

Spiral galaxy in the Andromeda constellation, also called the Andromeda Galaxy.

2.9 million light-years or .8 Megaparsec from your current position, end of information, shutting down."

A slight swirling occurs before the image fades out; the office slowly starts to be seen again.

Part 2, The Run!

With the cube still in his hand, Henrik's consciousness returns to the office, his head is spinning heavily. He feels fatigued, though he's in his chair, realizing that he never left it.

He re-orientates himself in the room, shaking off the weariness from the experience.

"What is this!? Where does it come from? Who is Viterin?"

The cube is dark again, he can feel the heat residue from it but it's no longer active. As he puts it down on the table, he closes his eyes as he leans back against the headrest.

The experience with the cube affected a part of his brain that has previously lain dormant; it activated memories of a distant place, a childhood memory that was hidden deep inside his mind. He is standing in the bottom of a valley, playing games with other kids, the valley is filled with long rust-coloured grass that is slowly dancing in the wind, bushy trees are spread around the landscape in groups, their structure is similar to some fungi on the ground. The top of the trees is round, seemingly compact, some have leaves that light up in neon blue, but most are green.

In the distance, he sees a woman with a beautiful, friendly smile standing on top of one of the hills. She is dressed in a white and blue-checkered summer dress who sends out a vibe of love and affection. She waves to Henrik and asks him to come to her, telling him that it's time for the birthday cake.

Henrik's memory is suddenly disturbed by the fact that Bjorn, his most trusted friend as well as co-worker, is grabbing his left arm as he holds one hand against Henrik's mouth so that he can't make any noise, with a slow and serious voice he says.

"Follow me ... fast, we must get out of here!"

Bjorn loosens his grip around Henrik's arm before he begins to move out of the room. Henrik swiftly gets out of the chair, for some reason he instinctively grabs the cube, puts it in his pocket and runs after Bjorn, when they come out through the office door he asks with a confused voice.

"Why are we running?"

Bjorn doesn't answer.

They run through an empty corridor, past the conference room, and out onto the stairwell leading

8

them down to the entrance floor, hopefully to a safe exit.

"Down the stairs, watch out for men in green coats, with some luck they have not turned up yet. quickly now!"

Henrik who is beginning to feel the rush of adrenalin in his body asks with an even more confused voice than before. "What men in green coats?!"

Bjorn suddenly stops in the middle of the stairs. Henrik almost stumbles over him, but is able to grab a hold on the handrail. They are nearly down to the second floor; Bjorn has seen something and both look down. At the bottom of the stairs, there is a large, well-built person in a thick, dark green coat and a short, peaked cap.

Even now, when he is standing with his back against them, he looks intimidating in his military stance. Bjorn gestures with his hands to turn around and go up again. They open the glass door to the office landscape on the third floor carefully, closing it even more carefully, trying to not make any sound. The desks in the office landscape are neatly lined up in sections of four tables in a square, with three sections on each side of the room. In the middle, there is a corridor with dark blue noise-absorbing partitions dividing the room in two.

Henrik notices that it's possible to see all the

way to the other side when standing in an upright position. Hiding behind one of the office desks, with a noticeable worried facial expression, "That did not work as I hoped for. We have to find another way out before they find us!" Bjorn said.

"Ok, Bjorn, but you have to tell me what this is all about! who are the men in green coats? What is this madness? Why are they looking for us?"

"We'll talk about it later when we are safe again. There's no time for explanations now, trust me, my friend." Bjorn looks around the desk for any of the men. "Think! Do you know any other way down not to mention out of here except for the elevator or the stairs?"

Henrik remembers that the old fire staircase is located on the opposite side of the room.

"I trust you. Follow me; if we manage to not get noticed through this office landscape, there should be a fire staircase that we can use. The alarm will be triggered, but my car is just a short sprint away when we get to the ground."

"Good, but we can't take your car, they have probably already installed a GPS transmitter in it," said Bjorn.

They move swiftly through the empty office landscape. The middle corridor is straightforward, with nothing between them and the door they entered, so they must be quick.

"Almost there now, check that no one has seen us," Henrik whispers

"The coast is clear ... no, wait ..." Bjorn said.

One of the men has spotted them through the glass door. He shouts something unclear at the same time as he pushes the door open before he starts rushing towards them.

Part 3, E.B.A.A.T

H enrik and Bjorn's feet move as fast as they can, with the man getting closer and closer to them. They reach the emergency exit leading to the fire staircase and kick it open with the brute force of someone who is being chased, rushing down at full speed without looking back. It's sunny outside; it's still early morning. On a normal day, Henrik would be outside on a bench, probably enjoying the summer sun while drinking a second cup of coffee, but this isn't such a day.

They run all the way to the ground, and when they take their last step on the staircase, Henrik, with his adrenaline-filled body, dares to turn around so that he can look up. What he sees surprises him. The man that chased them is for some reason not behind them anymore.

Maybe it's a trap...maybe they have us surrounded?... Henrik quickly shrugs off the thought as he feels Bjorn's arm pulling him forward so that they continue to run.

They run past Henrik's car, which is parked in front of his office.

It doesn't look like anyone has been inside it, tampered with it or put a tracker on it...but I don't even know how that would look like anyway...so...best to take Bjorn's car, Henrik thinks to himself.

After a few hundred meters, they cross the street and continue behind a corner of a different building, suddenly they can hear footsteps coming after them.

"They must be gaining in on us!" Henrik shouts with a voice that is both nervous and exhilarated.

"Faster! we can't allow them to catch us!" Bjorn answers while he simultaneously picks up an egg-shaped object. With a smooth movement, he rotates it around like an egg-clock, before he throws it on the ground.

"Quick! Run through the bushes over there...the object I threw will soon flood the nearby area with a strong knockout gas that will stop anyone who runs through it."

They swiftly make their way through the bushes, getting closer to Bjorn's car that he has hidden just behind a tiny concrete building, a dull, almost archaic electric substation with black air vents, that nobody ever notices.

When they reach the car, Bjorn says, "I believe

that we have managed to shake off the men from E.B.A.A.T. Hopefully, our escape will be smooth from now on." Both Henrik and Bjorn rapidly open the car's doors and get in.

Bjorn continues, "It looks like we're getting away this time. For a while there, I thought it was over for us. They are known to have backup plans, but they weren't really prepared for this, for you." They drive away, trying to take narrow streets until they feel secure.

"It's not the first time I've run from E.B.A.A.T, my friend. It has happened a few times during my life, but I'm surprised that it was so easy to shake them off. They can't have been more than a small group this time."

With not only a confused but also stressed and tired voice from the run, Henrik says, "EBAAT??... who are they? Why are they chasing us? What do they want from us?"

Bjorn gives Henrik a friendly smile before he reassuringly answers, "European Bureau Against Alien Threats, but you will get answers to all of your questions later, I promise. Let's rest for a while now, this is the beginning of your life, Henrik, your real life..."

Henrik doesn't notice, but a short pulse of gas has been sprayed directly into his nostrils with great precision, and his head feels unimaginably heavy.

Just before his consciousness falls into darkness, he manages to slur out, "... My real life? ... what...do you...mean?"

Part 4, The Awakening

H enrik wakes up with a pounding headache, feeling dizzy as well as disoriented. Carefully rubbing his eyelid with his palms, trying to open his eyes a little bit more. With a blurred vision, he sees that he is sitting in a quiet small room, on a white couch, in front of him is a fruit bowl filled with apples, bananas on top of something that looks like a giant peanut, but it is green, he thinks it looks soft.

" What happened?...where am I?... I have to get up on my feet."

The ceiling light is faded, but Henrik can see that the walls are completely smooth and white, the skirting and what could be a door framed with a narrow strip that slightly shines in green. The room is spotless. On the other side of the room, he sees a young woman sitting on a chair in front of a desk, with her back against him, wearing a white leather jacket, a pair of dark pants. Her hair is set in a long dark ponytail that waves as she turns her head while looking at the screens.

"H . . Hi . ." Henrik says with a trembling voice. No answer. "Hi, do you hear me?... Who are you?"

The woman doesn't react. She is wearing head-phones as she is focused on a big screen filled with line after line of unrecognizable symbols is scrolling down. Henrik slowly rises, feels how his feet find new balance on the floor, and takes small unstable steps forward towards the woman who has not moved from her chair. Suddenly, the strength of his legs vanishes; he collapses on the floor with a hard thump.

The woman jumps out of her chair as she calls for help.

"Dad! He is awake, come quickly."

Bjorn, who is just outside the room opens the door and runs in to see his friend on the floor. "I am so sorry, I was listening to music as I was going through the control system datasheet when he suddenly fell on the floor behind me," she says.

Henrik's vision begins to darken once more and before he falls into unconsciousness, he sees Bjorn and the woman, he feels them lifting him onto the coach again thinking, *Bjorn has a daughter?*

A few hours later, Henrik wakes up. His head is in

pain and feels awfully heavy. This time both Bjorn and the woman are in the room, Henrik has a saline drip attached to his arm, his legs still feel a little weird, but he manages to sit up.

"See who has woken up. You can relax, Henrik, we're friends, I promise that you're safe," Bjorn says with his greatest smile ever. "This young woman next to me is called Sofie, and she is my daughter."

Sofie smiles kindly to Henrik. He sees the similarities between them now: they have the same joy-filled smile, the same trustworthy face.

"Hi, Henrik, good to see that you once more are with us. We became a little worried when you fell. My name is Sofie; nice to meet you." She continues, still with a big smile on her lips, "You have to relax for a few hours now. Usually, it's a bit rough waking up after the anaesthesia, but you managed to hit your head quite hard when you fell so you need even more rest ... along with water, water is vital."

Sofie hands over a glass of cold water to Henrik, he takes it and drinks half of the glass in one go.

What day is it? I have to call my wife; she must be worried... Henrik thinks while he drinks the water.

"Do you remember that I said that this is the beginning of your real life?" Bjorn kindly asks.

Henrik nods as he tries to sit more upright in the coach, his head is starting to calm down.

"Are you sitting comfortably? Do you need any-thing before I continue?" asks Bjorn,

Henrik nods again before he manages to say, "Is Joanna alright?... I have to call her"

Bjorn understands his concern, so he tries to reassure Henrik.

"Do not worry Henrik, she is alright. We have an agent that will protect her if our green-coated friends dare to show up...we will pick her up as soon as you feel a little better my friend. Anything else?"

Henrik relaxes again as he hears this. "No, I'm good...I didn't know that you had a daughter, Bjorn. She looks just like you, continue."

"Good, I kept it a secret for you for reasons that will be obvious for you later. What I'm now about to tell you is something you can't prepare yourself for. It will probably sound too unbelievable to be true, but believe me, it's something positive." Bjorn puts an extra pillow behind Henrik. "Are you ready, Henrik? What a silly question to ask. How could you be ready for this? "

Henrik answers with a more confident voice than before. "Yes, I think I'm ready for what you've got to say, Bjorn...come on, just tell me now."

"What would you say if I said you were not born on this planet? ... that you're not even from this galaxy?"

Both of Henrik's eyebrow raises upwards making

his forehead wrinkle. With a perplexed expression on his face, he says, "I would probably ask you where the cameras are hidden..."

Bjorn gives him a short exhalation of amusement, a short laugh through his nose.

"You haven't forgotten your sense of humour, anyway...but it's true, I will let you process the idea in your head. Meanwhile, do you have the cube that stood on your table?"

"Yes, I have it in my pocket," Henrik replies.

"Good, take it out. Ask it for information about the planet Zuood."

Henrik picks up the cube, which is cold.

"How do I start it up?"

"Hold the cube with a firm grip in one hand. You can use the other for support if it feels better, then you just visualize your desire for what you want the cube to do. The first time you activated it, it scanned your brain structure, to be able to integrate correctly with you, simultaneously it downloaded information about your position before it updated its database, so it took some time ... now it should go more or less directly."

Henrik tries to visualize the word Zuood in his mind, the way the letters form the name combined with how it connects to a round planet. At first, nothing happens, but a second later, Henrik is standing on a hill filled with burgundy grass. The clouds move unnaturally fast in the sky, like a fast-forward on a movie. In front of him he sees something that could resemble giant seagulls flashing past him in circles around a giant blue tree, looking more like a hurricane than a flock of birds

Henrik can't move. His feet are planted in the ground as he tries to understand what has gone wrong. Bjorn suddenly shows up next to him.

"Hmm, something's wrong with the time perception setting. Everything is moving a little faster than normal, so to say. Let me change it."

Bjorn disappears briefly again as Henrik manipulates the cube in his hand. It's a somewhat unpleasant feeling, small vibrations in his palm, but after a minute the clouds and the seagulls begin to calm down. Henrik can now see that the birds that he thought were seagulls from far away, are, in fact, artificial; they act more like drones in the sky, hovering around as they gather fruit from the trees.

"Let's see, yes, this looks much better," says Bjorn when he returns. To the right of his field of view, a small information box appears with the text:

Planet Zuood.

Residents: 285 billion.

Area: Doova, lakevalley

End of information, waiting for instruction

Part 5, Kionidoo

The information box fades from Henrik's vision, and from the hill he sees a large city that at first glance resembles Manhattan or Dubai with its giant skyscrapers and dazzling lights. The city lies on an arch-shaped peninsula next to a wide river filled with turquoise water, and in the middle of the city there is a massive harbour. Most of the skyscrapers are interconnected, with several glazed passageways along the entire structure. It resembles an ant nest with about twenty floors between the passages.

"What is this city called?" Henrik quickly asks, trying to learn as much as possible about this new world.

Bjorn clears his throat before he can answer; he's thirsty. Before they entered the cube simulation, he had prepared a glass and put it on a table in front of him, so he takes the glass of water out of the air and drinks half of it before taking it out of sight once more, placing it back on the table.

Henrik laughs before he says, "That was a nice little trick you did, Bjorn."

Bjorn answers with a voice that is filled with warmth. "Thank you. She is a beauty, isn't she? Kionidoo is the capital of Zuood. The name is a combination of three words in an old, almost extinct Zuoodi language ... Ki means The, Oni means Turquoise, and Doo is the word for Lake. The Turquoise Lake or Kio for short." Henrik enjoys the scene playing before him. He sees giant boats slowly cruising the river, but there seem to be no waves after the boats, at least no visible.

Suddenly Bjorn starts to hover in the air in front of Henrik, slowly starting to move towards the city, turning his torso towards Henrik.

"Come now, just follow me...it's easy, just imagine that your body can fly," he says.

At first, Henrik is unable to lift from the ground, but after a few attempts, he manages to lift a bit in the air, laughing and thinking, *It's more or less VR, of course, I can fly* . . .

"Good, you learn quickly, Henrik." Both now fly rapidly towards the city and soon they hover over the turquoise water in the middle of the city.

Bjorn points his finger towards one of the buildings. "You see the tall building shaped like an arrow over there to the left? It is the city centre."

"Uhm...yeah what about it?" Henrik asks.

"You were born and grew up in there. You know I'm just a little bit older than you, my friend, and we spent a lot of our youth in there. We're not just close friends Henrik; in fact, you and I, we are cousins." Henrik smiles as he hears the answer.

"I'm glad you're my cousin, Bjorn, but why do not I have any memories of this? I got a short flashback after I used the cube the first time. I saw a beautiful woman standing on a hill waving to me, was that my mother?" They are approaching a balcony on the arrow-shaped building.

"Your memories are suppressed. You will most likely regain more memories in time, the woman you saw was probably your mother, Anvu. In a way she also raised me when we were kids; I spent almost all my time with your family."

"The balcony we approach, was it my home?" asks Henrik

"For a while it was, during some happy years. You will meet your mother when we arrive at Zuood in a month, but we must first repair the ship. After that, we can return to our dear home planet."

Henrik gets excited and happy that he will meet his mother, but he also wonders where his father is, as they touch down on the balcony.

"My father? I can't remember his name just now, but is he alive?" Henrik carefully asks.

"Unfortunately, he's not with us anymore, Henrik. Mato, as he was called, was an incredibly loved and cherished person for this city in the same manner as he was for the whole planet. He's dearly missed by everyone; he was a remarkable man Henrik," Bjorn says. Henrik had hoped that his father was alive. He has a faint memory of a man with a slim, muscular body with the biggest heart you can imagine, his hair combed backwards, a man who radiates calm, relaxed, and cool energy.

"In what way was he important to Kionidoo and Zuood?" Henrik curiously asks.

"A long time ago, in the aftermath of a more than fifty-year war between the planets near Zuood, a war of resources and power, At that time, your grandfather's father founded a power centre that consisted of several nearby planets, the Andromeda Alliance. Together they strived for a brighter future. A long time after that, your father founded Kionidoo. He held the position as the third president of the Andromeda Alliance until his death. Mato was a role model for many, an inspiration for generations of Zuoodes and the reason you and I had to flee from it all as young boys." Henrik nods as he carefully listens to every word that Bjorn says.

"Your father's political opponent, Tidus Barlow, the leader over the Chronos Corporation, had begun to gain ownership of more and more companies across Zuood. His only desire was to take over the power as ruler of the galaxy, and to achieve this goal he had to ally himself with an alien force, a race called Youll, from the nearby galaxy Triangulum." Bjorn takes a deep breath so as to gather his strength to be able to continue. "The sole aim of the Youllians was to ensure their own survival. Their share of power and resources, since their galaxy was in the midst of being destroyed by an unbalanced black hole that would rip Triangulum apart any day. Behind the scenes, they made their plans to overthrow the Alliance along with your father."

Bjorn pauses briefly again.

"On a day that forever will be remembered with darkness, they ruthlessly took over. Together with the Youllians, they managed to overthrow your father and wipe out the Andromeda Alliance leaders. Your father didn't make it out alive...I'm so sorry, Henrik."

Henrik stays silent for a while, processing the information he just received, before opening his mouth again to say, "It's not your fault, Bjorn. Don't feel sorry about the past; just tell me what happened after that."

"After the fall, Chronos Corporation took ownership of all companies on Zuood and removed any possible political opponents. To keep the people from revolting against them, they received a time dilation device from the Youllians. The device makes time run at a slower pace for the user, so you are able to work more and be more effective. The people of Zuood are poor and prices of living are very high."

Bjorn looks out over the virtual reality's preserved beauty of Kionidoo as he once more begins to go through the history of the alliance's downfall.

"The device makes it possible for the people to earn just enough money to make a living. Although some parts of society are better than others, the living conditions are for the most part ruthless. Do you see the beautiful, pristine, and turquoise river below, Henrik? That river has been transformed and neglected, polluted by waste throughout the years since Tidus took power. It's now brown and lifeless."

Bjorn falls into silence to let Henrik reply, Henrik is still looking down on the river below, going through everything Bjorn has told him. He decides that this is the wrong place to consider what happened to his father and the people of Zuood, he needs to exit the virtual reality and return to real life.

"What you have told me is outright terrible, my friend. We have to do something about this and get out of this simulation now, I've had enough for today."

"Of course, Henrik, I understand, all you have to do is think of turning off the cube. It will take care of everything safely and securely."

Both return to consciousness aboard the ship. Bjorn understands that it must have been much for Henrik to stomach, he feels that it's best to show him around the ship to let him adjust in peace.

"Welcome to the Starship *Eclipse*. The ship is just over two hundred and fifty meters long, and is designed to take us into orbit at any time, but now I will give you a tour. Later on, we will meet the crew on board. We are currently thirty agents in service, as well as a lot of robots, ranging from simple service models to our advanced androids. We are one of the surviving crews from the Andromeda Alliance. Everybody on board this ship are vowed to protect you, the heir of Andromeda."

"Heir of Andromeda?" Henrik gasps as he hears Bjorn's last words.

"Correct, Henrik, together we will take back what is ours, restore peace and prosperity in Andromeda. With your help, we will return the Alliance to its former glory," Bjorn answers with great confidence.

Part 6, The Tour

Henrik sits alone in the small, white room where he woke up, contemplating the situation and his role as a supposed heir of a far of galaxy that he apparently originates from.

How could this be? what do they expect me to do as heir? He has sent Bjorn and Sofie away for some time. He needs time for himself to let all the new information and his new situation sink in. It is difficult to process the fact that he isn't from earth, that he is in an actual spaceship, that spaceships like this even exist at all, that the ship's crew is preparing for take-off to another galaxy. But the most difficult to process is the fact that supposedly his new mission and purpose in life, as Andromeda's heir, is to take back control of Zuood. To take back what his father, his ancestors, created and fought for throughout generations.

No, Henrik has no clue at all how this is to be done.

He decides to walk out of the room, to find Bjorn, to let his thoughts process in the background.

Bjorn wasn't so hard to find; he was just outside in the corridor, sitting in a relaxed position on a chair with a footrest. Henrik watches him curiously. Over his lap, a holographic image displays some sort of mechanical part that he manipulates with one of his hands, writing very angled symbols onto a document. By the look on his face, he is in a good mood.

Henrik asks, "Bjorn, what are those symbols?"

Bjorn answers with a bright smile. "My dear friend, I'm going through the progress of one of my smaller research projects. The symbols you see are Zuoodi. Not so hard to learn, really, all you need to focus on is counting the angles and recognizing where the dots should be to form the letter."

Henrik just stares at the symbols with an expression that reveals his interest.

"You will learn later on, Henrik. Follow me, I want to show you the ship."

Henrik follows Bjorn through the long corridor. It is illuminated in a way that makes it look broader than it is. Along the corridor, there are several doors. Henrik thinks that it reminds him of a hotel's hallway. Bjorn points to one of the rooms.

"As you probably suspect, these are the crew

quarters and private spaces. Everyone in the crew gets one. The room to the left is the largest. It is yours and Joanna's private cabin; nobody comes in there without your permission. Try to open the door. Just stand in front of it and it will open automatically once it registers your heartbeat in addition to your face."

The door opens almost simultaneously as Henrik moves closer to it, and they walk in. The room is decorated in a similar way as their home, luminously filled with green plants in addition to a large bed. In one of the corners a humanoid robot is standing.

"The robot you see inside is one of our later more humanoid variants. He is called Tom and will be making sure that everything is in order for you."

"Is it common to have personal household robots on Zuood?" exclaims Henrik

"It used to be more common. Larger households can have more robots at their disposal; some have even become a natural part of the family," explains Bjorn before he continues. "Some of our most recent humanoid robots are so well-developed that they might as well be human. Much is being done about their rights. The majority of the population supports their full right as living, conscious creatures with the same rights as us."

They continue the tour, coming to the end of the

corridor there is a broad stairway leading upwards, next to two smaller ones on each side leading downwards.

"At the bottom, we have our shared kitchen and lunchroom. Should we go there first" The lunchroom was relatively large; he couldn't see any tables or chairs.

"To save space, we have placed the tables on the floor, if you want a seat, then sit down. At the same rate as you sit down, both tables and chairs go up to your position wherever you are in the room, convenient am I, right?" Henrik could only agree.

"Let's move on...the next stop is the engine room." They go up a floor and open a thick door into the ship's engine room. An elderly gentleman named Davood, chief engineer and responsible for the management of the engine, welcomes them.

"Hi Henrik, nice to meet you. I am happy that you found your way down here. Come here so that you can see the vibrant heart of this craft." Beside him, he has a large, robust robot that Henrik suspects manages heavy lifting, as the robot's hands are coarse and large.

"The robot is called M.E.R.E.S, which stands for Main Engineering Robotic Engine Supervisor, but I call her Mary for short. She helps me down here, making sure to keep track of the situation while I take some well-deserved rest." Davood gesticulates with his arms while showing all the devices and units for Henrik. He points to a grey cube, about one meter tall. On the sides of the cube there are handles that seem to be able to disassemble different modules or to easily check and replace broken components.

"This my friend, the main controller, is called the ZePad, the Zetta Paradox Detector. It works by pulling computational power from natural paradoxes in the universe to provide enough processing power to connect the ship's different systems. Without doubt, the strongest computational power on board this ship, though far from the strongest machine we have. It works in Zettaflops, that's how many operations a computer counts per second, how fast it can calculate. Earth's strongest only work in the Teraflops area, I do not understand how you can live with it really...I know that they are working on a computer that approaches the Yottaflops area but after that, we have to...seek further and see new opportunities like...the use of black hole processors..."

Davood clears his throat.

"But now I will not grind on about the computer, we can talk more about it later if you are interested, let me continue the tour."

Davood opens a lead and robust door into a small

dark room. All three enter and he closes the door thoroughly again. The room is warm, the air inside feels dry and heavy.

"In here I get the same feeling as if I were in a sauna, what is this room?" Henrik asks Davood.

In front of them, there is a wall that leans outwards, behind which one can distinguish a dim orange light, like a fire dancing around a big ring at a soaring speed.

"This is the observation room for the reactor. The light comes from our fusion reactor. What you see is the plasma inside the vacuum chamber. The energy from the fusion reaction drives four electrical generators, and from here we take all our energy for the ship's electronics, hyperdrive system as well as the coffee brewer."

Davood opens a door on the other side of the room which leads them into the engine compartment itself, the noise inside is deafening. A team of mechanics and service robots perform the work together. Side by side, they operate heavy machinery and lift huge parts into place, similar to how a resource factory operates.

Henrik sees three massive engines in the middle of the room next to each other. The middle engine is about double the size of the other two beside it. They are in the furthest part of the room. The engines are painted marble grey and have several large pipes along the sides.

"We are now in the ship's stern. The two smaller cylinders you see before you are our fusion rockets for normal cruising speed. The bigger one is our antimatter thruster, we use it for sub-light speeds. At the moment, tremendous maintenance work is being done on them. The parts are manufactured in our own workshop. In the next room, we have the control systems for the latest design of our hyperdrive, a propulsion system that places the ship in a parallel dimension where the distance to where we want to go is significantly shorter than in our dimension. When we reach the point that corresponds to the same point in our dimension, we jump back, but we have made some essential improvements. We have combined it with Tachyons, particles whose energy increases when speed decreases, and vice versa. For an exceptionally long time, it was uncertain whether the particle even existed, but we found it eventually and took control of it."

Henrik is absolutely fascinated. This is a beauty of the system, real engineering skills from a different world.

"Can you guess what Tachyon's finest feature is?" asks Davood. Without letting Henrik answer, he continues, "Their absolute lowest speed is the speed of light, so whenever we want, we create a field, like a bubble around us of these particles as we travel inside, which makes us able to travel at an incredible speed across the universe. We have not yet tested our absolute maximum velocity, but theoretically we should be able to travel hundreds of millions of light-years in just a few months."

"At what velocity does this ship usually travel?" Henrik asks.

"Depends on the distance in the parallel dimension we travel in comparison to our target in this dimension, but we will arrive at the Andromeda galaxy in about thirty days, so about four thousand light-years an hour."

"That's incredible! thank you so much for your in-depth presentation of the systems, highly fascinating," says Henrik. Davood wishes them a nice day as he immediately returns to his work with one of the major controllers. He draws out one vertical module that shines green and red before he disappears into another room.

Ascending again, up both stairs and up on the third deck, the bridge, and the control room.

"Come on, I'll show you the bridge. I am personally very proud of it," Bjorn said.

They walk through a short corridor that leads into a big room. The walls are bright white. The middle of the room, from the corridor and through almost the entire room, is raised about half a meter.

There they look out over the bridge's various sections. Some seem to handle external information, such as long-distance radar and course setting, while other stations take care of internal functions, like the life-sustaining system and the week's lunch menu. At the far end of the gangway, is the captain's chair; positioned in front of it rotates a three-meter-long blue hologram that shows the ship's status.

"The hologram that you see here provides visual information, and you can see all life forms aboard as well as an informational text that is displayed with a line showing you the path to interesting points. At the moment everything looks ok, except for the engine room that shows some red details because of the work down there. This information can also be obtained and displayed in a similar fashion at all times in the ship's quarters."

Henrik notes that there are a couple of small shuttles on top of the ship that he believes are used for shorter transports. Maybe they can pick up Joanna in one of them.

On both sides of the bridge, along the walls of the room, a few crewmembers sit in front of large control panels, monitoring different control features, displaying information on life-sustaining systems, regular inspection, the structural integrity of the hull, information about any errors or leaks.

"Say hi to the bridge crew, Henrik." Bjorn waves to them. They wave back, welcoming both of them.

"Hi, it will be a pleasure to meet you all later on so that we can get acquainted," Henrik said. while waving back. Along the forward-facing side of the room, all the way from floor to ceiling, through a large window you can see the outside of the ship along the second floor from here to the front, it starts to darken outside. It's time to call Joanna, to show her this.

Part 7, The Pickup

B jorn is sitting comfortably on the captain's chair, going through details of the work down in the engine room. Henrik is in front of him, studying the hologram of the ship, thinking about all that has happened during the day, feeling a duality in his mind regarding being the said heir of Andromeda, a tingling fear and at the same time a strong sense of curiosity towards taking on his new mission in life. To set his foot on Zuood for the first time, to work together with the Alliance to take back what once was his father's town, planet, and galaxy.

But first, he must let Joanna know that he is alright and will be back soon.

"I need to call my wife. She's probably worried, she hasn't heard from me all day, but what should I tell her, how should I explain?" Henrik wonders

"Just say the truth, that you have been with me

all of the day and was unable to call her. We'll explain everything later when she is onboard," Bjorn replies.

"Can we expect E.B.A.A.T to be there?"

"We can most definitely expect that. We'll land carefully behind the house, hoping they will not notice us. I will contact our field agent before we leave"

Henrik makes a short call to Joanna, who sounds worried on the other side of the line, but feels relieved that he is alive and well. He explains that he has been with Bjorn all day and has been unable to call her,

There is something wrong with her voice, Henrik notices, *best to act normal to not draw any suspicions if she's not alone...* He continues, saying that something life-changing has happened, that they will soon come home and explain everything.

"See you soon, honey, I love you. We have to get moving now," Henrik says before he hangs up the phone. "Something wasn't right, Bjorn! There was something in her voice that sounded very strange," Henrik says, with a worried voice.

"I know, Henrik, I am also unable to get in touch with Viterin, our agent. I think that we have to presume that E.B.A.A.T is inside the house and awaits us. Take this, you might need it." Bjorn gives Henrik a grey handgun that pulsates slightly in blue around the muzzle and along the barrel. Henrik takes the gun in his hands with a stomach-twisting feeling.

"Never fired a gun before."

"It's ok, Henrik, this is a pulse gun. It has three settings: pacify, kill, and incinerate. I've set it on pacify for you. This setting will only stun a person and I hope that you won't need it today. If any shooting occurs, let me take care of it first."

They both swiftly run towards the shuttle area, where there are four shuttles the size of a large van on top of *Eclipse*. One of the shuttles has been prepared already, so they get in. The inside of the shuttle is quite empty and the walls are dull white. The only thing that sticks out from the walls are two displays mounted onto the doors, one on each side of the shuttle. Along the side there is a foldable bench with seat belts. They get seated in the pilot and co-pilot chairs in the front.

"Buckle up," Bjorn says. The lift-off is not only smooth but also almost without any noise. Bjorn explains that the lack of sound is due to dampeners built into the engine of the shuttle. When they get to a reasonable altitude, Bjorn does something on the dashboard.

"I activated the shuttle's cloaking device so that no one will notice our arrival. We are now completely invisible to the electromagnetic spectrum and most sensors, or simply put, no one can see us...we will land in around five minutes."

The last five minutes feels like an eternity for Henrik. He can feel his adrenaline levels are rising inside him.

They land smoothly in the backyard of their house. Opening the shuttle door so that the light from inside won't be visible from the house, they begin to walk quietly on the lawn to get inside the house. From the outside Henrik gets the feeling that something isn't right. The lamps are off, and furthermore, Joanna is nowhere to be seen.

Why is it so dark inside the house? Have they... Henrik's thoughts are interrupted by Bjorn who grabs him by the arm to stop him from moving forward; he has seen something inside the house. Bjorn whispers to him to stay here as he slowly walks towards the house. Henrik can only watch while Bjorn moves to the terrace door with his handgun ready, slowly looking in through the window before he opens the door cautiously before he walks in, Henrik is still watching from the lawn, in a crouched position, seeing how Bjorn disappears into the darkness, everything is quiet.

A few seconds go by, nothing but silence, but suddenly Henrik witnesses three light pulses from inside in quick succession, three green flashes that fill the entire living room briefly in light. A shiver goes down Henrik's spine. After a few seconds, Bjorn appears in the doorway, giving support to a wounded, skinny-looking man dressed in a tight black suit, with one of his arms. He signals to Henrik to come in with his other arm.

Henrik feels the relief flushing down on him as he also sees that Joanna is standing behind Bjorn, he rushes towards them and when he reaches them, he grabs Joanna in his arms, holding her lovingly in a big tight hug. She asks, "What happened? Who were those men? They have kept me under watch for a couple of hours, not saying anything other than that they want to know where you two are...I was so afraid."

She's crying into Henrik's arms, shocked by the experience, but happy that they are alright. With a soft voice, Bjorn says, "I am so sorry that you had to be a part of this Joanna. I hoped that they wouldn't dare to enter your house, I saw three men inside; I pacified two of the intruders but one got away, we have to move quickly to the shuttle before he comes back. This is Viterin, he was sent here to protect you. He's hurt so we have to be quick now, follow me."

Viterin, with his slightly narrow bright lips, gives them a short, strained smile through the pain from the injury. His light blue eyes and thin face are adorned with a short, downy beard that makes him look much younger than he might be. He reminds Henrik of an old classmate that he thinks was from Canada, or maybe it was Russia.

Joanna feels more relaxed and safer now in Henrik's arms, a thought comes to her.

"Wait!...So you know who they are! Who those men work for!?" she says. Henrik still holds her in his arms, looking straight into her eyes he said.

"Trust me, my love, we will explain everything to you, but first we have to get into safety." She nods and Henrik grabs her hand. All four begin to make their way across the lawn. Bjorn is still supporting Viterin who has trouble to walking but manages to limp forward.

Bjorn stops in the middle of the lawn, standing next to the cloaked shuttle. The only thing that can be seen is a slight pressure in the lawn where the landing feet are standing.

"Why are we just standing here on the lawn?" Joanna asks, Bjorn points his arm right in front of him as he touches the shuttle door to open it. He walks in together with Viterin before he answers Joanna.

"We landed here, my friend."

Joanna's face morphs into a perplexed expression when she suddenly sees into a vehicle that shines slightly inside, but only sees what is shown through a door that somehow appeared from thin air. Bjorn places Viterin on the foldable bench, securing him tightly with a belt before he turns around again, looking back to invite Joanna with a friendly smile.

"Landed?" Joanna says, baffled, as she walks in. Henrik goes in last and closes the door again.

"It's a shuttle, my dear, best to sit down now. We'll go to a bigger ship and everything will be explained to you there," Henrik says as he buckles himself up on the bench. Joanna seats herself down beside him, tired after everything that has happened.

Part 8, Lift-off

O n their return to *Eclipse*, Henrik and Bjorn briefly explains to Joanna what is going on, and what has happened. Bjorn says, "Long story short my friend, sadly there is no time to prepare yourself for what we are going to tell you... those men that were in your house are from a European bureau called E.B.A.A.T, that monitors and takes action against alien threats found in Europe. That is the reason that we are all hunted by them..."

Henrik who is holding Joanna gently in her hands jumps in and says, "My love, as I said on the phone, something life-changing has happened," he continues to share the story of his and Bjorn's entire day. He finishes by saying, "...I know that it's much to stomach, my dear, much to process, but I hope that you will want to join us on our journey to our home planet, we will take off near midnight today."

Joanna who has looked deep into Henrik's eyes

with a remarkably calm facial expression during his entire explanation suddenly puts her hand soft against Henrik's left cheek and says, "I just knew there was something alien about you, my dear husband."

Both Henrik and Bjorn look at each other, amazed over her reaction.

"So...you're not surprised or afraid of the fact that I am alien and that we are about to travel to another galaxy? Not even a little?" Henrik says.

"I am a bit surprised, and I must say that I am a bit uneasy about going to another planet, but one thing that you should never forget my loved, is that I love you, I will always follow you, no matter what". She leans in to kiss Henrik before she continues. "If you aren't from this planet, so what?"

They all start to laugh.

Once back on *Eclipse*, they meet Sofie together with a team of medics that put Viterin on a portable stretcher and rush away with him to the ship's sick bay. Sofie is there to greet them and give Joanna a glass of cold water together with a warming hug.

"Hello Joanna, nice to finally meet you. I'm Sofie, Bjorn's daughter and the chief technician of the ship."

"Hi Sofie, considering the current situation it is nice to meet you too," she says with a big smile on her lips.

"Sofie is the most skilled technician on the ship. She has spent countless hours studying every corner of the ship. Her knowledge comes from her late mother, a beautiful lady as well as a talented technician on the ship, who sadly isn't with us anymore. Sofie was actually born on board, believe it or not...but now I want to show you all something, follow me outside for a minute," concludes Bjorn.

They all go into the elevator down to the ground and onto the meadow outside of *Eclipse*. It's night and the sky is filled with shining stars. So far out in the middle of a meadow, there is only minor light pollution, so that you can see the fascinating serene spiral of the Milky Way all over the sky. It is mesmerizing as well as breath-taking.

"If you look up in the sky," Bjorn points his finger up towards the stars, "Starting from Ursa Major, the two stars that form the back of the wagon. Imagine a line through these and then go down until you see the next strong star. You should now focus on the Pole Star in Ursa Minor, but do not stay there, continue down until you see stars that together form a W, it's Cassiopeia. Focus your eyes a little bit further away, there is Andromeda, there is your home, your galaxy, your Zuood."

As they follow Bjorn's instructions, they soon

lock their eyes at the shiny point in the sky that is Andromeda.

"I see it now. It's amazing to think that we will travel there. Thank you for showing us this, Bjorn," Henrik said while his sight is fixed on Andromeda

Joanna is speechless, unable to express her fascination with the idea of travelling to another galaxy. Bjorn hands her a phone that shows a picture of Andromeda close up and an old picture of Zuood.

"This is what it will look like when we finally arrive, now I think that Sofie wants to show you something."

Joanna turns around to hear what Sofie has to say.

"Every time I look up at it, I feel the same desire to travel there. I've never been there either, but now I want to give you the same tour that Henrik got from Bjorn so you can get acquainted with the ship and find out what's going on. Come with me now, I'll show you our amazing ship before we gather on the bridge for take-off." Joanna gives Henrik a kiss before she leaves with Sofie.

"Welcome to the Starship *Eclipse*. The ship is just over two hundred and fifty..." Sofie starts the tour, and they walk towards the elevator.

Henrik watches as they enter the elevator before saying to Bjorn.

"That was a close one, Bjorn. Let's hope that everything will flow smoothly from now on, I don't want to put Joanna at risk like that again."

Bjorn answers with a confident voice. "I can't promise you that this journey won't be free from certain risks, Henrik, but I can promise you that I will do my best to keep this crew, including you and Joanna, as safe as possible."

"I trust you. Let's go to the bridge." is all that Henrik can say right now.

They both take the elevator up and into *Eclipse*, talking about old memories. They laugh together when they remember that Henrik used to be really into old sci-fi movies from the 80s, but always thought that extra-terrestrial life wasn't something that he would ever see, that it probably would take thousands of years before mankind's first encounter would happen. Bjorn almost couldn't hide his urge to tease Henrik that he was one already.

About an hour later, Joanna together with Sofie arrives at the bridge after their tour. All preparations have been made now, both Joanna and Henrik begin to feel uneasy in their stomach.

"Do you feel the vibrations? It's the engines heating up. In a few minutes, we'll engage the lift-off."

They stand on the bridge looking out along the ship. With one hand they hold each other, with the other, they have a firm grip on the captain's chair. The vibrations get stronger and stronger until the ship suddenly leaves the ground and accelerates incredibly fast. Even with acceleration dampers both Henrik and Joanna get the same sensation as when they go up in high-speed lifts, the same heavy pressure, the same sense of weight and inertia.

After a few seconds, they reach the clouds as they continue accelerating. The sky is getting darker, and the acceleration feels less heavy now. After a while, they leave the inner atmosphere of the earth, and pass through the exosphere. The sky is now completely dark; the stars appear clearer than ever before.

Bjorn points out into the emptiness and says, "If you look at the left, you will see a relatively small white structure, it is your dear space station ISS."

Joanna gets a quick glimpse of the ISS before it disappears again.

"We will visit one of our biggest stations later on when we reach our destination, an intermediate station where we will pick up a dear guest."

Bjorn shows them the solar system on the way out before they shift over to hyperdrive.

"You will get a quick tour through your solar system before continuing to Andromeda. We will slide past the moon in a few seconds before we move on to Mars, Jupiter, Saturn, Uranus, Neptune, and finally, let's not forget your dear Pluto."

"That's amazing, could never believe this would happen when I woke up this morning," Joanna says. Henrik can only agree to that.

"We're just passing by Pluto, the last planet of this solar system. Do you want to see Voyager 1 before we get into hyperdrive?"

"Please take us there, it's not every day you get the chance to see it up close," Henrik says joyfully.

Not long after, they are cruising just behind it so that the magnificent little probe is visible through the window. The long mast taking the sensors outside the probes own magnetic field are interesting features, but the golden disc is what truly grabs both Henrik and Joanna's eyes; it's mesmerizing and enchanting. After they observe the lone probe travelling further and further away from the solar system for a few minutes, Bjorn sends the order to engage the hyperdrive

"You will notice that the transition feels a little sticky. It's nothing dangerous, it could be described as the feeling of taking a step back while blind-folded and simultaneously taking a deep breath that suddenly interrupts halfway in, it usually ends up with goosebumps all over your arms the first few times around."

Looking out through the large observation windows, Henrik says, "We are ready for it, let's jump."

Bjorn engages the hyperdrive. Henrik's sight becomes blurred for a minuscule moment, and then everything is back to normal again except that his hair is standing straight up. Bjorn and Joanna chuckle a little.

Through the windows, they see the faint Tachyon shell glimmering around the ship like an eggshell and it looks like they are travelling through a purple and blue cylinder with swirls around the walls like an intensive lightning storm.

"This is an astonishing sight, hypnotizing in its rhythm," Joanna says as her eyes are fixated against the outside.

Bjorn replies as a hungry person does, with only food in their mind, "The ship is more or less on autopilot now and I bet that you are hungry my friends. At least I am after this eventful day. There is a feast prepared in your honour, so let's get down to the dining room so that we can join everyone else."

The thought of food makes Henrik realize that he hasn't actually eaten anything except some fruit today. His stomach is more than ready to be filled.

They walk together down to the big dining room. It's crowded, and the room is filled with an amazing aroma from the food. Henrik smiles while pulling out a chair for Joanna so she can sit down. On the table is her favourite dish, lamb with steamed rice, and a fresh salad made out of cucumber, tomato, and red onion is served. Music starts playing in the background; the whole crew is in the room and the atmosphere is on top, Sofie stands up, whistles loudly to get everyone's attention.

"Dear friends, at last, we have Henrik and Joanna with us, let's welcome them the best way we can, let the show start."

In the middle of the room, a plateau is lifted half a meter from the ground to create a scene; four people in white bodysuits are standing silently in a ring, with their backs against each other. Their costumes begin to change in colour and pattern, slowly at first, then faster and faster, they begin to float, dancing and spinning over the plateau-like some kind of modern street dance mixed with classical ballet.

"This is a dance that tells us about our origins, from before we started travelling into space along with visiting other habituated planets," Bjorn explains to them.

The feast continues with laughter. Everybody comes over at least once to their table to present themselves. The crewmembers slowly start to leave the dining room, going to their cabins, filled with good food not to mention tasty drinks, deserving of a good rest after their hard work to get the ship ready for travel.

"I know that you are tired, that you need some rest too, but please follow me up to the bridge one more time tonight; there is something you need to see."

As soon as they reach the bridge, Bjorn disengages the hyperdrive to show Henrik and Joanna the Milky Way seen from far away. It is a wonderful mysterious feeling that is best described as an endless beauty, their entire view is filled up by the huge spirals that shine as strongly as the diamonds on Joanna's ring.

"What you see is your spiral galaxy. What do you think?" Bjorn asks

"That we are already so far away from Earth, from all our friends and family," Joanna answers.

Henrik looks towards his former home galaxy as he says with a voice filled with questions, "Yes, and our trip has just begun. I wonder what challenges we will face, how Zuood will receive us. I mean, my father was a popular man, but will I be able to measure up against the expectations that they most likely have of me?"

Bjorn hears his friend's doubt and reassures him that he will be fine. "The majority loved your father, but probably not many are familiar with you. Much has happened, we will introduce you with caution at first."

"Okay, you have to prepare me as well as you can during our trip."

"I will, I promise."

Part 9, Sabotage

T hey have been travelling for almost two weeks now. Henrik and Joanna are beginning to truly settle down in their new way of living. Every morning begins in the same way, with a breakfast in the dining room together with everyone else. After breakfast, they sit together with Bjorn as he describes the culture in Zuood, certain customs that are good to know to gain the population's trust as well as their votes. After that they work out, spending some quality time on the treadmill. They shower and then it is time for lunch. Some days, they volunteer to help one of the crewmembers with various tasks, to learn a bit about what the duties for the crew involve.

Today there isn't that much to do, so they walk up to the bridge to see Bjorn. When they arrive, they see that he is standing in front of the holoship. With a restless voice, he explains that he has just received an urgent message from Davood, that he needs to go down there.

"We're going to drop out of hyperdrive for a few hours. I have to go down to Davood to see what is going on, but please take this chance to admire the view if you want to, it's not often you get to see the universe from the middle of nowhere. We'll be able to jump into hyperdrive again in a few hours or so I hope, I have to go now, sorry my friends."

With that Bjorn starts to walk away from the bridge, Joanna and Henrik look at each other.

"Wonder what that was all about?"

"I'm not sure dear, let's take a look at the view, he will let us know if he needs us."

Bjorn goes through the door of the hyperdrive room where Davood works intensively with one of the modules for the hyperdrive.

"Davood, what's wrong with the system?"

"Unfortunately, I have to announce that we might have a saboteur on board. The system has been tampered with and without leaving any clear proof on who might have done it, the saboteur has managed to rig the system to crash three modules in the drive a week into our journey. Luckily, I noticed that something was not right and decided to control it all."

"A saboteur, who in their right mind could do such a thing!?" Bjorn furiously said.

"Can you fix the problem?"

"It will take time; I was able to locate the tampered modules and took the system offline before the entire drive crashed and burned," sighs Davood while he thumbs on one of the modules. "The person who did this seems to have profound knowledge of the system and has done their utmost to conceal any traces."

"Is it possible to reset the modules to full use?"

"Do not know, it will take time. We don't have all the components needed for such extensive repair, so I might need to manufacture most of them."

"Okay, do what you can, we must find the saboteur before anything else happens, meanwhile I will search for..." Bjorn gets interrupted by a call from Viterin.

"We need you on the bridge, captain, as soon as possible"

"On my way."

This is going to be a strange day... Bjorn thinks for himself.

Viterin has discovered an approaching ship. On the hologram a Man O'Warship is seen, data visualizing that it is over a mile long and fully armed.

"They sent out an automatic emergency signal, code Alpha-45, deadlock, what's your order, Bjorn?"

"Try to contact them, but first put us in a cloaked

state, shields at highest strength, and shut down the fusion engines, but have them ready. Our hyperdrive is currently out of order and this hardly feels like a coincidence. We are in the middle of nowhere and this ship appears...something isn't right."

"Yes, sir," answers Viterin

"Also, do a full external scan against them and alert the crew to get into battle positions."

Red lights start flashing all aboard the ship, a message alerting everyone about the situation is heard. Henrik, who has observed Bjorn's upset behaviour, decides to see what's going on. He approaches Viterin and Bjorn, who is going through the data shown on the hologram.

"The scan shows that the hull appears to be intact, no major external damage is seen, the scanning of the ship also shows that they are equipped with PDS capable weapons," says Viterin.

"PDS?" Asks Henrik

"Planet Desynchronizer. It fires a terrifyingly powerful x-ray pulse that blows away all but some electrons from every atom in a planet's core from the inside, leaving a void that begins to drain electrons from the rest of the molecules. Essentially, it quick starts a black hole in the middle of the planet, causing them to implode, nasty bastards."

"Shall we send a probe?"

"Do it. If the ship is abandoned, we can board, there may be parts on board that we need to restore our hyperdrive."

Henrik accompanies Bjorn and Viterin to a console for sending out as well as steering the probe. To the right of the console, through a window down the floor he sees it, it looks more or less like an arrowhead, approximately the same size as a small car. It's painted black, really black, so even in this light it's hard for Henrik to see any details; he perceives it more like a shadow.

"We call the material Vantablack. It absorbs almost all incoming radiation, light, micro and radio waves, made of nanotubes," Bjorn points out.

"The probe sensors can not only detect life signs, but it can also capture data transmitted on the ship's internal system. The colour is essentially unnecessarily discreet, but the design team decided it would stand out by not standing out," explains Viterin.

A cloud of dust combined with a swoosh sound is heard as the probe's airlock is opened. Viterin manoeuvres it towards the ship.

"Approach carefully and land on the hull, see if we can link ourselves to the ship's system and then show us the status on the hologram." Bjorn says.

On a screen, they follow the path of the probe as the screen creates a floating hologram that displays nearby objects in real-time.

"Now we should be past their shield, we are thirty meters from the hull ... ten ... five ... landed, starting up and scanning."

The probe tries to connect wirelessly and at the same time drills through the hull to connect itself to the ship's internal cabling system.

"No contact so far, no sign of life yet, residues of biological material, probably the crew, are spread in lumps throughout the ship. It probably isn't a pleasant smell on board, no idea what could have caused it."

"Report the status when the scan is complete. We'll prepare a shuttle in the meantime, there might be parts we can use or can help, so we should take the risk of boarding the ship," says Bjorn, observing the curious look in Joanna's eyes

"Joanna and Henrik, you're staying here this time. The risk is too great, there is no direct need for you to be on this mission."

They agree, even though their curiosity wants them to insist that they should join.

"Sofie ... Teem, I'll take you with me this time. Take three pulse guns from the armoury, just in case."

Viterin reminds them of the need for components.

"I'll ask Davood to send you the list, captain. I

think that you should try to board near their dock, I have studied a similar ship's drawings and with a little luck this one is similar, there should be almost direct access to the hyperdrive room from there."

"Good luck and be careful," says Henrik.

"You can be calm. With Teem on my side, nothing can go wrong. Teem comes from a long line of professional soldiers. She is the most reliable person we have on board, hopefully, no violence will be needed, but one should always be prepared for the possibility." Bjorn, Sofie and Teem turn to the shuttle. Viterin has just received the results from the probe responding.

"Obviously, the scan showed that the life-sustaining system is reduced to a minimum, only emergency systems are running, we can confirm the presence of robots, however, could not determine whether service or combat type... sending coordinates as well as a visualization of the appropriate place to board, be careful now."

Sofie sits at the control panel and starts the shuttle. A quick check of the system is made before departure, and they depart swiftly before they carefully move towards the large ship.

"It's an impressive ship, this one. It looks angry and full of confidence, built to intimidate." Bjorn comments on their way towards the dark and massive warship.

With an experienced and calm voice Sofie replies, "It's not intimidating me at least! I'll get us close to the hull before I activate the magnetic feet. We should be in the correct position in 10 seconds, prepare for the boarding." Teem sits at the shuttle's airlock, with a pressure suit on and a plasma weld in hand, ready to immediately go out and try to get up one of the ship airlocks opened.

"Just let me know when we are ready. I will do some magic on the hull." Just before the shuttle nudges the hull, Sofie activates the feet, and a loud noise is heard when metal hits metal while the shuttle is secured to the hull.

"Everything looks good. I activated drilling of explosion bolts against the hull so we are firmly stuck in case something unexpected would happen...Teem, you can open the lock, be careful."

"Always." Teem closes and locks the upper airlock door, she empties the small amount of oxygen contained in the cylinder and opens the door below her.

"Towards infinity and beyond..." she said as she pushes herself out of the shuttle.

"You do not have to be so dramatic, Teem, it's just another day on the job," laughs Sofie.

"Nobody has died from a little drama ... any information about when the ship could have been built? So, I know how complex the system I'm going to work my way around is."

There is a short silence before Viterin answers

"This can't be correct. Wait a minute, I have to double-check. The ship is at least from Andromeda, that I am sure of. It is time-stamped with the same blockchain as we use in our system, but the height of the blockchain is way too high. According to the timestamp it suggests that..." short inhalation is heard from Viterin as he gasps for new air to fill his lungs. "...If the scan is correct and the height of the blockchain is correct, it will be built about two hundred years from now, though the decay seems to indicate that it's at least fifty years since it left the dock."

Another inhalation is heard deeper this time.

"...So everything seems to point out that ... the ship we're facing ... that you stand on Teem...is... " Bjorn interrupts Viterin.

"Be extremely careful, it seems like we are dealing with something completely unknown to us. Everything seems to point out that the ship in some way can not only travel in space but also in time. This fact feels alarming and ... exciting, but we continue our mission. Sofie, you stay on the shuttle and make sure we can hurry away from here, blow the bolts now just in case."

"Ok, Captain, I'll put all systems on standby. With just a jerk on the controls, I can accelerate with full force away from the ship."

"Good... Henrik..."

"Hear you loud and clear."

"If for some reason, I do not come back, I trust you to ensure stability in our system, you have the people behind you."

Henrik feels the responsibility weighing on his shoulders, he does not know what or how he will stabilize an entire galaxy, but he put the thoughts behind them at the moment and answers

"I will not let you down."

Teem is heard over the radio. With a sarcastic tone she says, "Can I do my job now... or are you going to continue your emotional conversation? You'll get tears in my eyes."

The Man O'warship's hull has probably seen better days, she notices while she is navigating to the airlock she will try to open, Sofie and Bjorn observe her progress.

"Be careful, Teem, we do not know if the Androids inside are a threat or if they are aware of our presence or not."

"Understood, almost there now, keep you updated, this will be a big challenge."

Considering the fact that the ship is both old and not even built yet, the system will probably be different from all the other systems that I worked with during my days... this will take time. Suddenly she sees how something moves to the right in her field of vision, far away, gas explodes out of several gaps in the hull.

"Do you see that? The oxygen is being dumped from the ship! I suspect our presence is known. We must be extremely careful when we enter. Viterin, have we received any response from our attempts to communicate with any intelligence on the inside?"

"Nothing new yet, we repeat our call every ten seconds."

Teem is almost thrown out of the hull when a gap suddenly opens just before her.

"That was a close one! I'm at the airlock now, beginning to work my way in."

She begins to cut through the airlock plates. Once she is finished, she carefully enters.

"I'm in! I can report that the ship's artificial gravity is out of order, what are your..." Before Teem finishes her sentence, a muffled sound is heard over the radio

"hrz hra hrz borgh"

Part 10, Rescue Mission

N o other sounds are heard from Teem's position. A few minutes have already gone by with silence as the only reply. Bjorn is standing ready to go outside, trying to contact Teem over and over again.

"Teem, can you hear us? Report back." Nothing.
"Teem!.."

"What just happened? Who or what made that noise?" Sofie asks through the radio.

"I'm not sure, but we will check...Viterin, do you have any visual?"

Viterin who has been watching everything on both the hologram as well as on a video feed, didn't see much. He has put the event on a loop, searching for details that can uncover Teem's fate.

"I'm going through the event, Bjorn, but I don't have good enough of a visual inside the ship. Teem's life signs are still there, but the signal is getting weaker, her heart rate is normal, so I think it's just interference inside the ship."

Bjorn gets down into the airlock and closes the lid above him.

"Assemble a rescue crew and prepare them to be ready to depart with a shuttle on my command, let me know when that is done. Meanwhile, I will get out and peek inside the airlock that Teem opened. Sofie you stay sharp here in the shuttle in case we need a quick retreat back home."

Bjorn pushes the button that vents the remaining oxygen in the airlock chamber and opens the door as he activates the magnetic shoes he is wearing. Once he is down on the hull, he moves as fast as he can towards Teem's position. The hull is dormant, no more oxygen is being pumped out, so the short distance to the airlock isn't hard to complete.

Henrik feels that he should be included in the rescue team, to engage and show that he is reliable, he talks with Viterin about it, demanding to be included.

"I volunteer to be a part of the resc…" Before he can finish his sentence Viterin answers.

"Good, I have no problem with that. I have prepared a list of other volunteers and skilled persons. I'll let them know that you'll join them, go down to the armoury so that you can get ready, hurry."

Surprised by how easy it was to convince Viterin

to let him join, Henrik rapidly walks down to the armoury. There, he meets the team. There are four other crew members in the room who volunteered for the rescue mission. He recognizes one of them from the dinner a few days ago. He found out that his name is Moktai and that he is from the south, from a small farm village south of Zuood's equator.

Another familiar person in the room is Loukh a short man with a large moustache. Henrik worked together with him a couple of days ago and he noticed then that he is the kind of person that doesn't talk that much. As they worked, Henrik found out that he utters words only when he finds it necessary. Loukh believes in action more than words, or at least that what was he said one time before he handed Henrik a wrench to help with some minor adjustments in one of the engines.

Henrik puts his spacesuit on. He finds the suit is surprisingly easy to move around in, not more hindering than when wearing skiing gear. The boots are comfortable but quite heavy, they have to be with the large magnetic sole that keeps them fastened to the hull when walking outside.

As it's Henrik's first time putting on a spacesuit, he is a bit unsure on how to put the rest of the gear on and struggles with the helmet.

"Let me help you with securing the helmet. It's too bulky to put on without knowing the trick to what goes first." Moktai says.

"Please do, it's hard to see if it's fastened correctly or not."

Moktai lifts the helmet and the oxygen tank over Henrik's head before he fastens it down. The helmet and rebreather, combined with the oxygen system, is built into one item, with a shielded hose connecting the small tank and the helmet.

He flips the switch for the radio communication before he steps back and asks Henrik to say, *"HUD on."* to activate the Heads-up-display.

On the helmet's visor, Henrik can now see important data, such as who is speaking, how much oxygen he has left, how the rebreather system is operating, and whether the suit is sealed.

"Thank you, are we ready to go to the shuttle now?"

"Almost, take this." Moktai gives a pulse gun to Henrik, who puts it in his holster.

Bjorn who has reached the airlock turns on his helmet flashlights, turns off the safety on his pulse gun and takes a careful look inside the ship, just turning his head slightly so that he can peek inside, the door inside the airlock is opened, so there is no pressure inside the dark corridor of the ship.

"Will they be ready to depart anytime soon?" Bjorn asks Viterin

"Yes sir, they are ready, do you want me to order

them to depart?"

"Do it. Tell them to land next to my shuttle and come to my position. We are going in."

Viterin sends the order, and the shuttle is soon on its way. He turns his radio to a private channel between him and Bjorn.

"One thing that I didn't mention, Bjorn, is that Henrik is onboard the shuttle, he insisted on being included in the rescue team."

Bjorn quietly smiles inside his helmet before he can answer, this is exactly what he wanted to hear.

"Great, I'll let him know that it's ok, this could be a greatly dangerous mission, but if he insisted then I suppose that he got a reason for it."

The rescue team lands and the crew of five quickly walk outside. As this is the first time that Henrik has experienced the vast emptiness of space first-hand, it is making him feel a bit sick. He looks up and there is absolutely nothing but emptiness above him. He only wants to get inside the ship's airlock so that he at least has walls surrounding him once again. He walks next to Moktai, who speaks with a rich, powerful voice, even when he only engages in small talk.

He sees that Henrik isn't feeling well and says, "First time out on a spacewalk is a gut-wrenching experience, I know, just take one step at a time, look at the ground and you will feel better. Now come on, we better get to the captain quickly."

Henrik does as he said and begins to feel a bit better. Soon they reach Bjorn, who stands just beside the airlock.

"Good, it's great to see that you take charge and start thinking like a leader my friend, this pleases me, let's walk carefully inside and find Teem. We have heard no new sounds through the radio and no attempt to contact has been successful, we must assume that she is in danger, but we will bring her back alive."

They walk inside. Joanna and Viterin observe their movements with worried eyes. Bjorn goes first; the corridor is only lit by dim emergency lighting, so they must use the flashlights to move around. They go past the airlock doors and move further into the corridor. Everything looks out of order on the inside, Henrik almost stumbles over some loose cabling that is just lying on the floor.

"What could have happened in here?

"Not sure, we better move carefully further in. Stay behind me."

They continue walking. The corridor looks the same all the way: there is some kind of dark-red organic material everywhere on the wall and the floor, and they walk past a few broken doors with nothing but more mater inside.

"Try to avoid the substance on the floor. We

don't know what it is. No sign of Teem yet, so keep your eyes and mind cleared; we are getting closer to the control room now," Bjorn says.

When they reach the end of the corridor, they find a half-opened slide door. Bjorn peeks inside the opening. It's quite dark inside and the room is only lit by a few blue coloured lamps. From what he can see, it appears to be a large room filled with control modules built into shelves in the room. In the middle of the room there is a control panel with blue lights. Standing next to it is a droid that starts to go past the control panel. Beyond Bjorn's visual and behind one of the shelves, there is more organic material spread out in the room in chunks.

"This must be it...Moktai, open the door carefully. There is a droid inside, we will cover you," Bjorn whispers through the radio. Moktai turns off the safety on the pulse gun and opens the door with one hand. He walks in, the others following just behind him.

Part 11, Belly of The Beast

As they enter, they see that the room is completely filled with the same organic material they have seen throughout the corridor. The walls and floor are cluttered with piles of the material.

"Be careful. The droid could still be here somewhere," Moktai says, just before he sees Teem sitting on the floor on the other side of the control panel. Her head hangs down and she seems to be unconscious. He quickly moves to her to check if she's alive.

"She is breathing but unconscious. Help me get her up on her feet, it looks like she has a tiny hole in her suit. Her oxygen levels are dropping. We need to get her out of the ship and into the shuttle fast." Moktai waves with his hand for someone to come while at the same time trying to wake her up.

Henrik quickly moves to help him with Teem. When they lift her, she regains consciousness, and with a fatigued voice, she tries to speak.

"..the droids..they are..they.." she breathes trying to clear her head.

"Save your energy, Teem, we'll get you out of here, it was a good thing that your magnetic boots still worked so you at least stayed grounded." Moktai and one of the other team members walk out of the room with Teem, taking her to the shuttle.

Bjorn is trying to turn the control panel on. After a few seconds, it lights up and the holoscreen shows a list of the ship's video log entries. Bjorn inhales deeply when he sees the Chronos Corporation logo in the middle of the screen.

"We are in the belly of the beast; this ship is marked with Tidus' logo," he almost whispers it out, since he knows what this implies.

"According to the vlog, the last entry was made about one week ago, at least in this ship's origin timeline which in the Gregorian calendar is around the year 2268. I've connected the sound feed to my suit and streamed it to you so that you too can hear what the captain of this ship said. I've already made a backup of the ledger to our drives so we can further investigate this later on," Bjorn says as he navigates down to the last entry. "I'll play the latest vlog first"

A man wearing a black captain's suit appears on the screen. He looks exhausted, and his face is sort of wet. He speaks with a rough and fatigued voice.

"Captain's probably final vlog. I am Kirkoo, the date is Z 273,5,15. Death is upon us...if someone ever sees this, let me explain what has happened... two weeks ago we engaged our hyperdrive.." Bjorn pauses.

"The captain is in agony, something is clearly wrong with him, maybe we should be glad that we are still in our suits." he resumes the vlog.

". . . there was a fault in the hyperdrive mechanism. It's unknown what caused it, but we were sent back in time...we checked against the stars to be sure. We encountered an unknown substance when we travelled in hyperspace and somehow it entered the ship. It spread out like fungus in every corner of the ship and made everybody very sick... it's like nothing we have ever seen before and any attempts of eliminating it only made it stronger." The captain grabs his head with both hands, he looks even worse now than before.

"...only a few of the crew are still alive, including me, but I fear that we too will see the darkness before the day is over. We are heading towards earth, remember us...the true winners of the fourth great war..." The captain walks away and the vlog ends.

Bjorn stares down at the floor, contemplating on what the captain means with the fourth great war, he will have to go deeper into this later. Henrik and the others stare at each other. They now know that they can't just re-enter the *Eclipse*, but have to be quarantined until they are certain that they are safe to enter once again. Henrik is feeling an ice-cold sensation as he goes through the fact that the ship is on a slow journey towards earth. They must stop it from ever reaching its destination.

"We have to..." Henrik is interrupted by the same weird noise they heard before, similar to radio disturbances.

"hrz hra hrz"

"Get behind cover, something is coming towards us, hold your fire until we know what it is," Bjorn orders and they gather behind the control panel, ready to fire at whatever is coming.

There are four possible entries for anyone or anything to get into the room, but only two of the doors are visible from where they stand.

Suddenly they see one droid coming in from the same door through which they entered the room. A shadow is seen from the other side of the room and another from behind them. Bjorn sees that they are surrounded and orders them to fire, they must surprise the droids before they open fire themselves.

Henrik fires the pulse gun at one of the droids and the entire room is lit up by the pulses from their guns. The droids are moving fast towards them now. Filled with adrenaline and fear he misses at first but hits the droid with a few shots that were enough to remove its threat. It floats in the room due to the lack of gravity.

Bjorn almost gets hit by the return fire from the two remaining droids that have entered the room. With the help from Loukh, they manage to disarm one of them, hitting its weapon and then vaporizing the last droid.

"The threat seems to have been handled for now," Loukh says with a short and unemotional tone.

"Everybody ok in there?" Viterin asks through the radio.

"I think that we are fine, nobody got hit at least. Our oxygen levels will soon be depleted, so we have to be quick here now," Bjorn answers.

"Find the parts and get back to the shuttles quickly, meantime I will find a way for you to be decontaminated for return."

"We have to find the modules and rig explosives on the hyperdrive and blow this ship into a million pieces. The needed components are added to your suits' HUDs', search the modules for them, but be careful, there are more droids probably on their way down here now."

They spread around the room, with their gun in one hand and going through modules with the other.

"Moktai, get back here with some explosive charges, hurry."

"I'm on my way captain," Moktai answers.

"Good." Bjorn switches over to a private channel with Viterin.

"Viterin, try to download as many of the vlog files as you can before we blow this ship up, we have to get a greater understanding of what the great war that the captain mentioned was all about."

"Yes sir, I will do my best."

Henrik takes out module after module in search of the parts that are needed. The suit HUD helps him by giving AR recognition if the parts are compatible or not and if someone already has filled the needed quantity of parts. So far, he has found one module that is complete and can be used and a few parts that he has taken away from other modules. After a while, they have collected everything they need and gathered around the control panel once again.

During the search, Moktai arrived with the explosives and together with Bjorn they have located where they need to go to access the hyperdrive engine.

"We have to move quickly now. I've started the warm-up phase on the engine and set a countdown of thirty minutes before the engine is engaged, so we need to plant the explosives and get as far away as possible. We have to go two doors back down in the corridor to find the room that has access to the engine itself. Moktai and I will place the explosives and start the engine to maximize the blast before we detonate the explosive charges, the rest of you will take the modules quickly into the shuttle where Sofie is sitting ready to depart and return to *Eclipse*. We are all low on oxygen levels."

Henrik understands exactly what Bjorn is implying: he is uncertain if he and Moktai will be able to return and therefore will not put further risk on the crew. He is astonished by the true leadership and courage Bjorn embodies.

"One of you takes the modules and parts, the rest provide necessary cover fire, move out now and be careful," Bjorn continues. They all begin to walk out of the room the same way that they entered. Moktai goes first and sees that in the corridor everything is as it was before. They quickly reach the hyperdrive engine door, Moktai enters and secures it, making sure no droids are present.

"Make sure that you get back to safety my friend, I'll see you again shortly, we have a mission to complete," Bjorn says to Henrik before he joins Moktai in the room.

Henrik nods and says, "See you soon my friend."

Henrik leaves with the rest of the crew. The corridor is abandoned, and no droids are seen, Henrik is carrying the parts and is following Loukh towards the exit.

He turns around to face Henrik and with an unusually friendly smile, he says, "We will soon be back in the shuttle. Don't worry, I will cover you if needed."

Henrik only nods as answer and wonders what the smile was all about, but decides that it was nothing and moves on.

The journey back to the shuttle is swift and without any hostile contact. They reach the shuttle, where Sofie is ready to depart. She reports back to Bjorn and Viterin as soon as everyone is buckled up.

"We are ready to depart. Everyone is on board and we are ready to depart on your order."

Bjorn answers and feels a good sense of relief that at least some of them will make it out alive, as he is not so certain about his and Moktai's survival chances.

"Good, get back to *Eclipse* as fast as you can; we will join you shortly."

Bjorn and Moktai are standing on a bridge right above the engine. The room was in fact a service entrance with only one bridge in it that goes from

83

wall to wall, with the engine directly beneath them. They can see other bridges further away, but other than that, the room is uninteresting to look at.

"The engine is huge, but where can we plant the explosives?" Moktai wonders.

"We have to find any hatch that puts us closest to the core of the machine. Jump on and open any of them, we have to just try and hope that we have some luck. I'll cover you." Moktai jumps over the railing and onto the engine and starts to open as many hatches as he can. On the private channel, Viterin contacts Bjorn.

"Captain."

"Yes, Viterin, a bit of bad timing now, but go ahead."

"I've good and bad news sir. I've figured out a procedure to get you back inside *Eclipse* safely, so that is more or less cleared now, sir. That was the good news, the bad news is that thanks to Davood, we have identified the saboteur. It's Loukh and he is with Henrik. Please advise."

"Loukh?! Are you sure about this?" Bjorn questions.

"We have definitive proof that it's Loukh, sir, his fingerprints are all over the place and we found schematics in his private quarters."

"Let's not say anything just yet. Watch over Henrik and observe them through the video feed from the shuttle, alert him on a private channel if needed, otherwise just let them back on board after they are cleared and secure Loukh. If required, you are allowed to take him down."

"Affirmative. I'll let you know if anything happens, good luck with the explosives and come back alive, over and out."

While Bjorn was talking, Moktai finished with the explosives and climbed back up onto the bridge again.

"I've planted the explosives on three different positions, sir. Let's get out of here now."

"Follow me. We are almost out of oxygen now, only got a few minutes left of air, so we really need to hurry."

"Understood."

They walk out of the room and move as fast as they can back to the shuttle. They are only one hundred meters away from the airlock and their air should be just enough to get back to the shuttle.

"Watch out," Bjorn says as he sees a droid coming out of one of the doors on the left side of the corridor. He opens fire and hits the droid, who now floats lifelessly in the corridor, but behind them two more droids appear.

"We have to get out of here. Do as I do," Moktai says as he disengages his magnetic boots, bends his knees, and aims for the airlock, Bjorn does the same, and they jump together, moving swiftly in the corridor. Flashes of the droids' pulse gun rounds are passing by them.

"Prepare to engage the boots again; we are almost there," Moktai says with an adrenalin-filled voice. Just as they activate their magnetic boots, Bjorn hears Moktai screaming on the radio, having been hit by a droid's pulse gun. His suit is ripped apart and he is vaporized almost in an instant.

Bjorn is shocked and almost crashes into the airlock door, but he manages to connect to the floor and stop his forward movement just inches from the airlock and runs outside. He reaches the shuttle before any droids appear at the airlock. He quickly departs and announces the loss of Moktai with a deeply tired and sad voice.

"With a deep sadness and great gratitude, I have to announce that Moktai, who with bravery rarely seen and an ingenious quick mind just a few minutes ago helped me escape the Chronos Corporation ship alive, has left us. His last action alive was a showcase of bravery and he will forever live on in our hearts." He shuts off his radio for the rest of the journey back to *Eclipse*.

"I need this moment to honour him."

Bjorn lands his shuttle on *Eclipse* and orders Viterin to move the ship away before the automatic detonation happens. With full thrust Eclipse begins to put the Man O'Warship behind it and after only a couple of minutes, the ship explodes with a very bright shockwave.

Part 12, Loukh!

Bjorn is sitting silently inside his shuttle, thinking about Moktai and Loukh, contemplating the differences they have and what could have driven Loukh to betray them all.

"At least we now know who did it," he says to himself before he turns on his radio and contacts Viterin.

"Viterin, I just needed a minute or two alone with my thoughts. Have you detained Loukh and put him under guard?"

Viterin, who was going through the final stages of the decontamination results and was booting up Bjorn's process, was relieved to hear Bjorn's voice again.

"Yes captain, good to hear from you. We have him under guard in an empty sleeping quarter and have prepared the interrogation room for you when you are back inside."

"Good, I know I can expect a lot from you, Viterin."

"Thank you, sir, I also want to let you know that the decontamination process will begin in a minute or two and will take you around five minutes to complete."

"It will be a relief to be able to leave this shuttle. I expect that Davood has received the components by now. Tell him to report back to me with his progress, I want us to continue our journey as soon as possible."

"Will do, sir."

Henrik, who was shocked when two guards detained Loukh for treason and took him away when they left the shuttle, is now sitting together with Joanna in their private quarters.

"I don't understand, how come I didn't see or sense that Loukh had an agenda of his own? I'm truly shocked by the fact that he is responsible for the malfunction of the hyperdrive. I even worked side by side together with him a couple of days ago. Did he know that the Man of war ship was going to coincide with our path? Or was that just a coincidence?" Henrik says with a tired and puzzled expression.

"My love, don't be too hard on yourself. Even Bjorn misses this fact and he is the captain of this ship. Let us wait and see what the interrogation uncovers. Sometimes people can be experts at hiding their agendas from each other." Joanna takes his hand and they continue to discuss the matter as Henrik slowly begins to regain his confidence.

"You are truly amazing, my love, you can show me the sun where there are only dark clouds to be seen, thank you," Henrik says with a soft voice.

"Thank you, love, let's go down and meet the others."

They walk down to the corridor outside the interrogation room where they meet Davood, Bjorn, and Viterin.

"Good, everyone is here now, I know you are all tired after this tiresome day, so please walk in through the left door and observe. After this, we can hopefully get some rest," Bjorn said before he and Davood enters the interrogation room. Henrik, Joanna, and Viterin enter through the left door and find a room next wall where they can observe the interrogation through a see-through mirror.

"The room has only been used a few times under Bjorn's leadership, and never before have crew members had to be questioned," Viterin comments.

They can see that Loukh is already seated and handcuffed. The walls inside the room are deliberately painted grey and boring and the only items in the room are a metal table and two chairs. Bjorn seats himself on the second metal chair on the other side of the table, facing Loukh and with calm and relaxed energy, he begins to talk.

"First of all, I would like to say that you are sitting here because you are one of the crew members who possess the knowledge of carrying out the sabotage and that in your cabin, we found drawings and notes on how to implement it."

"Yes, yes that's right," Loukh says with a relaxed voice while slowly nodding his head in approval.

Bjorn continues, "As you probably know, this room is equipped with several sensors that measure the truth level in everything that is said in here, even what I say is measured and noted down."

Loukh sighs impatiently and says, "Yes...I know... please start asking your questions now so that we can get this over with."

"We don't want to spend more time than necessary, so let's start."

Bjorn leans backwards, putting his left leg over the right leg in a comfortable position. This is a part of his interrogation strategy, as he learned a long time ago it is a game of the mind and not so much a game of trying to force the truth out of the suspect. It's easier to let the person feel that the game is over when seated in a relaxed position.

"Do you have anything against the Andromeda Alliance?"

Loukh knows that his fate is sealed and he will be imprisoned until they arrive at Zuood. He refuses to admit to Chronos Corporation's command that he has failed his mission, but he has a backup plan and knows that these will probably be his last words, so he relaxes and takes a deep breath. *Why not let this old sack find out just how much I am against it, and that they will be defeated, one way or the other.*

"Yes, and I'm not the only one who shares my belief. We are many," he finally answers.

"So, you did sabotage the hyperdrive?"

"Of course I did. This was only part one of my plan, but I was interrupted."

"Interrupted by the other ship you mean? Did you also know that the ship would appear here?" Bjorn quickly asks. Loukh only smiles.

"Actually not, but it was a pleasant surprise. I know how dangerous and how powerful that kind of ship is and hoped that they would blast us all into smithereens."

Bjorn is starting to feel his disgust with this man flood his veins, but shakes it off without showing it. Henrik is truly surprised with the attitude that Loukh is showing and the way that he is speaking. He no longer talks with the same voice as before and he certainly isn't just talking when it's needed. This is more like bragging about what he has done and planned to do.

"You said that you are not the only one who shares your beliefs. Is there anyone else in this crew that wants to damage the Andromeda Alliance?"

Loukh puts his right leg over his left leg, mimicking Bjorn's position to show him that he isn't afraid.

"You would like to know that, wouldn't you?"

Bjorn slams his fists onto the metal table, knowing that this fight isn't over, and the interrogation will take a long time.

"We will end here for now, but you will answer in time." He gets out of the chair and walks out of the room together with Davood. After the door closes behind them, he asks Bjorn why he ended the interrogation so quickly and abruptly.

"Why did you lose control in there?"

"I didn't, I just let him believe that he got to me, this will take time and to continue right now would only waste everyone's time and energy for nothing. We have to soften him up a bit before we continue," Bjorn answers with a completely calm expression. Davood nods understandingly. Bjorn signals to the guard who was standing outside to take Loukh back to his quarters before they enter the observation room where Henrik, Joanna, and Viterin are standing.

"What did you think about his reactions and comments in there my friends?" Bjorn asks.

While they have their focus on the discussion on the interrogation, the guard is about to escort

Loukh out of the room.

"Come on, move it, traitor." Loukh has no desire to do as the guard says, so he reaches out towards the guard. His hands are still handcuffed but he manages to take the guard's weapon out of the holster, and shoot him in the back.

The guard doesn't even have time to react before he falls on his knees and collapses like a sack of potatoes. Loukh drops the weapon and runs towards the door and out to the corridor.

The others hear the gunshot and are shocked as they see the interrogation room. Joanna is the first to run out of the room and chase after Loukh; the others are just one step behind her.

Loukh runs as fast as he can towards the shuttle area but is abruptly stopped after he rounds a corner and one of the guards manages to take him down.

"Let me go! The Alliance will fail ... no one ..." shouts Loukh before the guard injects him with anaesthesia.

"Check if his signature delivers any affiliation with Chronos. Check if Loukh actually is his real name or not, then lock this traitor under strict surveillance in his quarter until we reach Andromeda and can put the traitor before trial!" Bjorn says to the guard.

"Signature?" Henrik asks with a curious expression.

"All citizens are injected with a chip at birth and a DNA stamp containing a unique code that both are checked against a blockchain ledger for confirmation, about where they are born and other necessary personal information. Imagine the same function as a birth certificate. It's located in the right hand and it's pretty neat in my opinion" Bjorn explains.

"Ah, I understand. Can it be used for other purposes as well, Bjorn?"

"Of course, my friend, the data describing you are locked, but the chip contains a rather generous amount of memory in order to cryptographically encrypt any important information you need. You can store a cypher either in your head or on another device to gain access to the data. It's pretty handy for the most part." Bjorn chuckles loudly at his unintended pun, they begin to slowly walk up towards the bridge.

Later in the evening, a meeting is held in the lunchroom, which contains a depressing lack of energy. The mood is low while Bjorn and Henrik talk about what has happened.

"Loukh's motive was that he believes Henrik is not entitled to any power at Zuood. He would have stopped at nothing to make sure that we never arrive at our destination. His ruthlessness cost the lives of two brilliant people, Moktai and Ziigot, who will never be forgotten, let's share a moment of silence."

While everyone is in the lunchroom, Loukh wakes up and succeeds in escaping from the sleeping quarter via a hidden air vent that he has made sure would be a way out if he ever was caught, without hope and without seeing another resort. He finds an airlock, gets inside it, closes the door and breaks the control panel before he manually opens the door outwards, disappearing quietly into the darkness of space.

Part 13, Halfway There

The disappearance of Loukh leaves a lot of questions unanswered. His disappearance was noted the next morning, when the guard was to take Loukh to the interrogation room for another sit-down. The whole crew was involved in the search and every corner of the ship was covered until they found the damaged airlock wide opened. Bjorn declared Loukh as deceased and the work on repairing the hyperdrive and all other normal routines onboard could finally continue.

Later that day, Davood and Henrik are down in the engine room, working together to get the hyperdrive engine working again. They have, together with M.E.R.E.S, double- and triple-checked the system to make sure that Loukh didn't leave any unexpected surprises left on any module or in the software. Henrik has started to enjoy working with his hands down in the engine room and feels that the work gives him time to reflect and think about the topics he and Bjorn are going through every day. He is beginning to find at least one foot firmly landed on the mission to reunite the Andromeda Alliance.

Davood sees that Henrik is a little stressed

"It was a rough day yesterday, but I hope that the next few weeks will be a little bit calmer, how is preparation for our arrival at Zuood going?"

"It's a lot to learn and a lot to think about. We are going through how the Alliance was formed and who the former leaders were. It's interesting and important that I understand the past to be able to make the correct judgement for the future, but first we need to arrive at Zuood, how far have we come do you think?"

"Indeed, the past is crucial to understand, especially if you are supposed to lead us into a brighter future, young heir," Davood says. Henrik smiles and rolls his eyes as he hears Davood calling him young heir, Davood notices and smiles back before he continues to talk.

"We should arrive in about two or two-and-a-half weeks if nothing interrupts our journey. We have a stop on the way on one of the larger stations, but after that, we are almost in Zuood's backyard."

"So, we are about halfway there now, more or less? It's incredible how far away from Earth we have travelled so far."

"You will get used to it. Hand me that module if you are finished with it. Let's get the hyperdrive operational again."

Henrik had finished with the module he had on his desk, Davood takes it and slides it into the final slot on the system. A beep is heard, and the system awakens with a faint blue light that is shown through the distance between the different modules.

"Start the test procedure that I've prepared. Just press the button shown on the screen."

As Henrik does that, different parts of the hyper-drive engine are shown on the screen in a wireframe view. One part or module is tested at a time at first, then the entire start-up and a simulated test drive are done.

"Everything looks blue. Nothing in the red zone, so I think that we are finally good to go," Davood says as he inspects the results and exhaled in relief before he continues.

"Report back to Bjorn and see if he has anything else for you. Maybe we can be on our way now. I need to rest awhile; not as much energy in me these days, maybe I'm getting old," he says before he seats himself down on one of the chairs behind the workbench.

"I will see you later Davood," Henrik says as he leaves the engine room and walks up to the bridge, on the way he goes through the events that have happened up to this.

What a different life we live in today, hard to believe that we are in between two different galaxies right now, Henrik thinks as he walks with a smile on his face, they will finally continue on their journey.

When he enters the bridge, he sees that Bjorn is standing near the holoscreen with Viterin.

"Hey, we are good to go; the system is up and ready," Henrik says with a big smile on his face.

"Good work my friend, we need to talk, but first let us engage the hyperdrive so that we at least are on our way again."

"Captain to all crewmembers, prepare yourself for hyperdrive propulsion mode," Bjorn announces through the radio before he activates the hyper-drive.

Henrik asks Bjorn about what they heard from the captain's vlog. "I've wanted to ask you before, but the opportunity never arrived, the fourth great war? What was that all about?"

Bjorn and Viterin share a quick glance at each other.

"That's actually what I wanted to talk about. This will probably sound bad, but as we know it, we believe that the ship was coming from an alternate dimension, so the final story isn't really certain just yet."

Viterin continues where Bjorn left off. "After going through the vlog's content, we now have a tiny glimpse into a possible future, some parts are good for us, others are a bit..."

Bjorn jumps in again. "Let's say that if this future as we saw through the vlog will come true, then the Alliance, with I assume your help was not only revived but was strong. We had kicked out Chronos and for some years the rebuilding of the Andromeda Alliance, peace and prosperity were once again something to be sought after in the galaxy."

Henrik smiles, astonished at the fact or possible fact that he was able to complete his mission. He says, "Well that's great news so far but, what about the war?"

"Let me continue. We didn't see anything mentioning when they had joined the Alliance, but Earth was a small part of it, which is why the Man O'Warship was heading towards the planet." Bjorn takes a deep breath and slowly exhales, letting the air slowly leave his lungs before he begins again. "The Alliance thought that Chronos Corporation was history by now; sadly it wasn't. Chronos backed down, but wasn't abolished as we understood it. Tidus Barlow, their leader, finally took his last breath a couple of years after we took the power back and Chronos was thought to have been permanently gone after that, but around 150 years later, a small group revived Chronos and in secret built a war fleet that was finalized after fifty years, who now terrorized the Alliance planets. A long and drawn-out war with losses on both sides was once again disturbing the peace in the galaxies."

"I see, so this could be seen as a lesson for us when or if we are able to take back power and control over Andromeda?"

"Could be, or it could just show us the reality from that dimension, which could might as well play out differently for us. One thing we can be sure about, one thing that probably will be the same, is that Chronos will not back down easily. We will have to work hard to unite the Alliance and to finally take back the power."

Henrik nods in agreement, and has one more question in his mind. "What was it that killed the crew? Have we been able to analyse the material?"

"Unfortunately not. Everything was scrubbed clean during the procedure in the shuttles. Let's just hope we aren't affected in any way," Viterin answers.

"I understand...so what's next?"

"We will arrive in around two weeks. We need to make one stop on the way as I mentioned before, to meet a friend."

"I've heard a lot about our planned stop, but I've never heard anyone mention what is there, or who we shall meet."

"We will visit the Odyssey station, located on the outskirts of one of the super star clusters, not so far away from Zuoods star system, I think you will find it interesting my friend"

" One of our local agents who is deep undercover in Chronos government should meet us there and grant us clearance to travel closer to Zuood, if not then we can't disguise ourselves as merchants, that's our way in, I hope."

"A fragile plan that could easily fail," Viterin adds

"Fragile indeed, but it's probably our only way in at the moment that at least has a chance to succeed."

"We'll see, let's discuss this further at a later time, but now, let's get something to eat. I believe that my wife is waiting for me down in the lunch-room," Henrik says.

Part 14, Odyssey station

A round two weeks has passed by. Henrik and Joanna are back to their daily routines, filling their days with learning about the history of Andromeda, working out together in the gym, enjoying delicious food with the crew, and on the afternoons joining in with Bjorn and Viterin at the bridge, as they discuss on how they will achieve their goals. It is late in the afternoon and they have just finished for today with developing their plan as Bjorn makes an announcement on the ship's intercom.

"We are closing in on Odyssey station, going out of hyperdrive in ten minutes. Your two-week-long rest is almost over. It's almost time to start the next chapter in our story."

Henrik and Viterin walk over to Joanna, who is standing at the front of the bridge looking out through the window as they come closer to Odyssey station.

"It's an impressive sight," Joanna says as they look with awe upon the station.

Viterin answers with a voice that makes him sound just like an experienced tour guide who is still just a little bit impressed by what he sees. "It surely is. The design is taken from older stations; they are calling it retro design. As you can see, it is built with a dual torus-shaped design that consists of two separated torus rings spinning in opposite directions to each other. The upper one is used for plant cultivation and the lower one is storage facilities. The metal, dome-shaped structure above is packed with an impressive arsenal of weapons. It's more of a fortress than a station in that way."

He pauses for a second before continuing.

"If you look below the torus rings, you see that the docking ports are organized so that each shuttle easily can approach and depart without generating too much confusion and traffic."

Around and all over the station, several ships are either sending out shuttles, receiving cargo or are stationary. There are movements in and out of the station at all times.

"This is probably the most visited station, since it is located so close to Zuood and every ship needs to have approved clearance from this station to proceed towards the planet," Bjorn says.

"It's an amazing sight," is all that Henrik can say as his eyes go from one ship to another. The larger vessels are mostly dark in colour and heavy looking, giving the unmistakable impression that they are freighters. Henrik's vision focuses on a group of five that catches his sight. They are a bit closer to the station than the freighters. They are painted bright white, triangle-shaped with a large blue double helix symbol along the entire hull, before he even has time to ask, Bjorn answers his question.

"Those vessels mean trouble; they are Youllian patrol ships. Usually, they scout the area for any possible smuggle routes that some scavengers use to get their scrap materials sold on the shadow market. Let's hope we don't have too many encounters with the guards; they aren't afraid to demonstrate their authoritative powers," he says. "The double helix symbol represents the duality between Chrono and the Youllian empire, or something like that." Bjorn raises his eyebrows and shakes his head in frustration before he returns to the control pad.

Bjorn tries to open contact with the station control.

"Captain Bjorn on *Eclipse* with crew, requests

docking permissions for two shuttles, signing transaction now, over."

"Transaction confirmed, use ports Y-4 and Y-5 and await further orders," the station replies a few seconds later.

"Let's go to the shuttles and begin our next step in our journey," Bjorn says with a light and enthusiastic voice.

"Joanna and Henrik, you are with me, we'll take one of the shuttles. Sofie and Viterin you take the other, prepare it so that we can use it in an emergency if we need to depart very rapidly from the station."

"Yes sir. We'll begin the preparations immediately," Viterin answers.

Seated in the co-driver seat, Joanna watches as they slowly approach one of the gates. A large sliding door is opened; the floors and walls inside the large docking bay are painted completely white and she sees that there is a control room further in.

"Fun fact," Bjorn suddenly says, "This bay is built for the mid-sized shuttles. They built the different sizes to accommodate different needs. We got this one since they scanned our shuttle size and model." The shuttle slows down and the landing feet are secured to the floor in the bay.

"One guard is standing in the control room, ready

to come out as soon as the bay is re-pressurized. He will go through our papers and then a standard search procedure will be done, nothing to worry about. If anyone asks, just state that we are a cargo vessel seeking further permissions from the station to approach Zuood and they will hopefully not bother you anymore." Bjorn says.

Joanna and Henrik nod and at the same time and say, "Understood." Henrik smiles at her.

"First time we are on an actual space station, my love."

The guard leaves the room and walks towards their shuttle. He looks like a tired old man, wearing a slightly worn-out uniform, ready to retire.

Bjorn is the first one to get out of the shuttle, walking down the short ramp on the back of the shuttle. While he hands over his papers, he says, "I know you are going to ask, and no it's not my first time at the station. I'm frequent visitor here, you have my member key on the paper."

The guard doesn't give away any emotions when he scans the paper with his control pad and confirms it with the ledger.

"Everything checks out. You are free to leave the shuttle and wait on the designated area until the scan is complete," he says as he points his arm towards one of the corners in the bay.

Joanna and Henrik leave the shuttle and follow Bjorn to the area the guard pointed out for them, the guard enters the shuttle and pushes a button on his control pad. A blue and green laser scans the shuttle, going from one end to the other. The guard comes out again, walks over to Bjorn and says, "You are cleared, stay within the permitted zone and welcome to Odyssey."

Bjorn takes the paper that is handed back to him and they begin to walk towards the bay exit door.

"Sofie, report your status."

"Sofie here, our bay is still being pressurized; meet up outside the bay in five minutes or so."

"Good, see you soon."

Bjorn, Joanna, and Henrik walk out of the room and through a tunnel that automatically scans their body as they pass through. The area outside is filled with people, busy with their daily work and business. An enormous energy is sensed through the masses as they see people selling food and services, the ceiling is set high above them, and Bjorn starts to give them a little background information regarding the station.

"This is the Odyssey market. It takes up the rest of the space on this level. The market is divided into four different zones: food, clothing, technology, and miscellaneous services. There is also a residential area. It's always crowded, and pickpockets are known to roam around sometimes," Bjorn explains. As he is done, he sees Joanna and Viterin entering the area from the door next to them.

"Good, now that we are all here, we can begin our search," Bjorn adds.

"I want to look around the market for any parts that we might need to stock up on, I'll take Joanna with me. Is that ok, Bjorn?" Sofie asks.

"Sure, feel free to look around while we search for our friend, we meet up here in about two hours. Just remember bay Y-4 and Y-5 and you should come back here easily. Shall we go, my friend?"

"Let's do it," Henrik says as he gives Joanna a warm smile before he wishes her luck and gives her his concern.

"See you soon, love and be careful." They move into the crowd and disappear.

"Let's have a little adventure on our own," Sofie says with a spark of excitement in her eyes and before Joanna can answer, she adds, "Before we search for parts, I want to see if I can find Gox, an old friend who hopefully still has his bar near the technology area. Let's see if he's still around."

"Sure, I'll follow you," Joanna answers just as Sofie grabs her hand and off they go.

They quickly move through the crowd. The technology area is at the other end of the market. On the way Joanna sees a lot of differently dressed people and glances at the merchandise that is sold. People bargain and shout to each other. The market is a mish-mash of different stores, some better developed than others, using holodisplays that show commercials about their products and offer walk-in stores. Others look more simple and basic, using paper signs and simple tables to showcase their products.

Suddenly her glance gets stuck at one particular person. She sees an unusually long and well-dressed figure wearing an elegant dress that almost touches the floor, with a broad and silky scarf hanging down from the neck. The person's face is smooth and in a light tone of blue-green, but the eyes are completely orange.

Without slowing down, Joanna asks Sofie.

"Who or what is that?"

"That is a Youllian. Don't look too long at her or you will draw too much attention. They have a reputation of being ruthless, thinking that staring is offensive," she answers and pulls Joanna further into the crowd.

Soon they reach the bar that Sofie talked about.

"Here it is, hope that he is here."

They walk in. The bar wasn't as crowded as Sofie anticipated, but there are a few people inside, which looks like mostly older men and a couple of younger Youllians. The light inside is dimmed down, and all the decoration is glowing in neon colours, glowing blue ceiling lights, and sparkling green tables combined with muffled music that is played in the background. The bar is lit up in a bright white tone.

They approach the bartender, who is a stylish-looking middle-aged man wearing a white shirt that reflects the colourful decor of the bar. They order one drink each and Sofie takes the opportunity to pass him a note with the name Gox written on it and a question mark. The bartender reads the note as he serves them their drinks. He begins to nervously look around the bar before he leans towards them and with a voice trembling with concern, he quietly whispers, "Don't ask me about him. He is not here, probably in his flat. Don't look for him."

"May I ask why we shouldn't look for him?" Joanna leans in over the counter.

"He is in trouble, they are looking for him, he owes them a lot of sats. I can't say anything more than that, please stop talking about it him now."

"One last question, who is looking for him? Who are they?" The bartender doesn't answer, Joanna looks around the room. No one seems the least interested in them or appears to be eavesdropping.

"I hear you, thank you for your answer," she said before picking up the drink and smiling towards Sofie.

"Let's get out of here after we are finished with these drinks. It would look suspicious if we just order drinks and leave right after. Is there any way we can figure out which flat is his?"

"Not sure, we can ask around a little discretely, I guess," Sofie says with a tone in her voice that lacks her previous sparkle. They drink up and leaves the bar.

"Where is the residential area, maybe someone can show us his flat there?"

Sofie begins to walk down the road, her mood is down, and Joanna notices her distress.

"Do not worry, we will find him in the end. Who is this Gox person to you, Sofie?" she asks as she walks beside Sofie.

"Gox is my oldest and most trusted friend. It worries me that he is in debt and in trouble, it isn't good to be in debt in this place...things happen."

"I understand, perhaps we can help him out?"

"Maybe," she quietly replies.

"But first we have to find him."

Part 15, Gox!

S ofie and Joanna arrive at the residential area. They have walked silently for some time, hoping that Gox will be there. The residential area consists of a large gateway binding together several corridors. Joanna finally breaks the silence and says, "Maybe someone is around that we can ask. Let's walk inside and see if we can find anyone."

Sofie nods hopefully with her head as they enter one of the long corridors. On each side they see numbered doors, around seven meters apart. Other than that, the corridor is silent.

"It's empty here. Maybe everyone is at the market right now," Sofie says.

"Maybe, but let's just walk around a little bit, with a bit of luck we should find somebody to ask," Joanna says confidently.

After a while, the numbered doors are replaced with more open spaces. They enter one of them, a dining area and kitchen.

"There, I told you we would find someone to ask in here," Joanna says when they see an old lady sitting down on a bench, going through something on a pad. She seems to be deeply concentrated on what she is reading and isn't taking any notice when they approach,

"Excuse me, we are looking for a friend, his name is Gox, Galdur á Gox, do you know where he lives?"

The old lady points her hand back to the corridor and says, "You find his flat in the second corridor, number forty-seven, but I don't think that he is still around."

"Thank you."

When they find Gox's door, number forty-seven, they see that it isn't completely closed.

"That's weird, why is it opened?"

"Hello? Gox are you inside?" Sofie says with a loud voice, hoping to receive an answer, but no answer is heard. She sees a dim light coming from inside, opens the door completely, and they walk in. When they enter, they see that the place is trashed, the furniture is broken, drawers emptied, literally everything in the flat is scattered on the floor. They round a corner and into his living room.

"Noo," Sofie yells as she sees Gox's body lifeless on the floor. She begins to run towards him, but Joanna reacts before she reaches him and grabs Sofie around her waist to stop her

"Wait, we need to contact the guards before we do anything to disturb the body, I'm so, so sorry, but we have no other alternative."

When Sofie has calmed down a bit, Joanna leads her out of the flat, holding her hands, they find their way back to the old lady to contact the guards. Sofie collapses on one of the chairs next to the lady, her head is spinning and she can't believe what she just saw. She hasn't told Joanna or anyone about how she actually knew Gox, how close they were to each other. After a while, two guards arrive, by the look on their faces they aren't surprised that something has happened in the residential area of the station.

They approach Joanna, with one hand on their holsters

The old lady sees it and comments, "No danger here, relax-"

They ignore it and one of the guards says, "What has happened here?"

"Our friend is in flat forty-seven, we entered and found him lifeless on the floor, he is murdered, from what I saw it looks like he is shot in his back. We left the flat as soon as we saw him, you need to report it."

The guard raises his left eyebrow, he isn't too eager to listen to what is in his opinion nothing that anyone else than a guard could determine.

"First off, little lady, we will take a look at his flat. You will take us there, and one of us will do the investigating part of the job. Secondly, we will take your statement later on." The guard takes a breath before he continues. "You are hereby under arrest, you will be able to contact your captain later on and until you have been cleared by me or anyone above my ranking you will be considered to be guilty." Big inhale and exhale this time. "Thirdly, I will only do this investigation if you approve this signature with your universal ledger wallet. If you don't comply, you will be charged guilty and will be sent directly to the airlock, since by law I and any guard are the law here."

Joanna finds her stomach to be turning, she hasn't been in a situation like this before, and starts to feel her heartbeat pulsating in her chest. She takes a deep breath to find her inner strength. As she does so she realizes that the guards are only portraying their power, believing that they can boss around them only because they are women. Now her blood boils, she fixates her eyes on the guard.

"I demand that you follow us as soon as my friend is able to stand on her feet again, and I also demand that you find the one responsible for this bloody murder. You will not detain us, and I will not sign anything until this situation is under control," she says, feeling her anger rise.

The guards, who aren't used to these kinds of demands, almost take a step back when they realize that their attempt to intimidate didn't work out. They also quickly realize that their jobs might be on the line if command hears of this, as the new management does not take harassment lightly.

"We'll do as you say," he says.

The other guard comments, "When she is ready, we'll leave. Can we start over? A new beginning so to say."

"Just find whoever did this to Gox," Sofie finds the strength to say with a voice filled with anger and sadness, her face is pale and red at the same time, she forces her legs to support her as she stands straight-backed once again. "Let's go!"

Sofie takes lead. Joanna and the guards follow her back to the flat, once there she orders them in while she remains outside, unable to look at Gox as he is right now. Joanna watches and makes sure that the guards do their duty, that they act accordingly and takes note if they find any clues to who might have done this. They search his body for any sign of violence.

"Look at this," one of the guards says.

"Beneath him was a piece of paper, marked with the Youllian signature, the black hole galaxy."

Joanna returns to Sofie quietly, so that the guards won't notice.

"We might be on the search for a Youllian. Do you know anyone that could have had business with Gox?"

"Of course, why didn't I think of it? Last time I was here, Gox mentioned something about a newly found investor." She is silent for a second before she continues. "We need to revisit the bar and get more information out from the bartender before the news is out that Gox is dead. We have to gain his trust somehow, is it possible that you could get the paper they found beneath him?"

"I'll try."

Back at the bar, they find the man lurking outside on the back, he is hurt.

"You two again? What do you want?" The man struggles to stay on his feet.

"Relax, we just want to talk to you."

"Last time we talked I got a massive hello from a couple of brutes, so excuse me if I'm not so happy to oblige you with further assistance." He sits himself down on an old box and begins to massage his hurt legs.

"You will help us, Gox is dead, and we believe it was one of the Youllians who did it, we have semi proof." The bartender laughs.

"Semi proof? I can tell you who did it, even point him down for you, but it won't help you anyway.

It will only bring pain to all three of us and most likely the end result will be the three of our bodies floating around outside the station. But yeah, sure I can do it, if you have a death wish, look inside the bar through the window and you will see a group of Youllians. The smallest of them is their leader, but don't judge him by his size; he is ruthless."

Sofie peaks inside and sees the group laughing together. They are playing some sort of game. Octagonal cards are dealt between them, two with their backside visible, two throws and one more card is dealt out, the first to draw a losing card is wiped out.

"Let's find the guards so they can arrest them," Joanna says.

"No, we will do something else. We will wait until they have taken their last drink and then we will take the leader out the old-fashioned way, with brute force equal to what they focused on our newly found friend the bartender," Sofie suggests.

"Ehm, I do have a name you know, it's Hudseon."

"Nice to meet you, Hudseon," Sofie says.

Part 16, Answers!

Sofie and Joanna prepare themselves outside the bar. They have found a few different objects that they can use to attack and defend themselves with.

"You will definitely need something to knock the leader down with. He is called Hurol," Hudseon comments as he sees them looking for anything that can be used as a brute weapon.

They wait until their game is over. With a bit of luck they can ambush Hurol when he is alone and away from his gang for a second or two. After a while, the Youllians finish with their game and are on their way out, laughing and walking unstably as they cheer the leader as their winner. Sofie hears them calling, "Number one Hurol, number one!"

Hurol is going to the bar to grab one last bottle before he too walks out to the gang. Sofie sees the opportunity and swiftly rushes in from the backdoor, Joanna is right behind her. She knocks

Hurol hard in the back of his head so that Hurol makes a grunting noise before collapsing on the floor.

"Great, now what?" Joanna asks. Sofie looks at her with cold eyes that could have been made of steel and iron.

"Now we make him talk, and record everything he said..."

They take him to the backside of the bar, Hudseon opens a door that leads further in and out to a storage room.

"We don't have much time. The gang will soon notice that something has happened to him. Call the guards right now and tell them to control the area."

Sofie does as he instructed and calls the two guards they talked with a few hours ago.

At the same time, Joanna secures Hurol's hands and feet with a rope and points a pulse gun against him, just in case.

It doesn't take long until he wakes up, his eyes have shifted from orange to a more velvet red hue. A stream of slow dripping blood is running down his neck from the hard bash from Sofie's hands. He just stares at them for a while, not even trying to break loose from the ropes. He is calm on the outside and it is as if he hasn't taken a single sip from any kind of bottle.

A few seconds go by without anyone saying anything, until Hurol opens his mouth and with a dry voice says, "What have we here? Who are you and what do you think you're doing? You know that you won't come out of this alive, right? And no one would ever dare to ask me if I had anything to do with your early deaths."

"You don't scare us, Hurol. We have some questions for you, and you will answer them," Sofie says, trying to sound as bored and imperturbable as possible by his attempt to threaten them.

"Alright young lady, I have to admit that you have some courage to speak to me in that way, I can respect that," he says as he lifts his thick and heavy eyebrows approvingly. "But it won't change the inevitable end for you all. What do you seek?"

"Why did you kill Gox, Galdur á Gox?" Sofie asks.

Hurol looks amused and a bit surprised by the question.

"That fool?! He owed me a lot of sats and couldn't pay up when it was due. He had gambled away everything, even his own bar, which I now own." He chuckles to himself before he can continue. "When I saw that he was prepared to try an escape, I simply removed him from my stack of unwanted, I shot the coward in the back"

Sofie raises her arm and gives him a jawbreaking punch, so fast and so hard that Hurol's head turns all the way to the right.

"Just so you know, we have recorded everything you have said, and I will personally make sure that you get the correct sentence for what you have done, your days out in the wild are done." is the last thing she said to him before he passes out again. "Joanna, please call the guards and tell them to collect one scumbag."

Shortly after the call the two guards arrive, surprised to see Hurol on the ground.

"We have been looking for you two, whatever happened here stays here. We don't want to get involved; we will take him to the station now," they guard says. Soon after the guards have placed him behind bars, Sofie turns to Joanna.

"I will stay here for a while, at least until his sentence is determined, then I will join you once again on Zuood. Thank you for helping me with this, I am forever grateful, couldn't have done it without you."

Joanna smiles.

"But now, maybe we should see where the others are, they must be worried, we should have been at the gate several hours ago."

They leave the bar area and walks towards the gate, exhausted and feeling ready to take a well-deserved rest.

A few hours earlier, Bjorn and Henrik had met up with the agent. They found him outside near the technological area. The man is as big as an ox, at least double the size of Henrik, with long beard, trimmed and formed similar to a snowplough on an old earth locomotive. They have moved up to the first torus ring to discuss in private and are now standing in one of the storage compartments; there are boxes stacked everywhere.

Bjorn instructed Viterin to stay a bit behind them and follow them, so they would have a backup in case something happens.

"So finally we meet, Henrik. I'm Rahu and I've heard a lot of rumours about you. Luckily, I don't really take gossip into such great dimensions."

Henrik isn't surprised that rumours are roaming around about him.

"Hope it isn't too bad at least," Henrik says, trying to sound funny.

"Nah, don't listen to rumours, that's what I've always thought."

"So, we hope that you have finalized the details in our papers Rahu and that you can give it to us, your reward will be transferred automatically as soon as your side of the contract is fulfilled."

Suddenly, Rahu's voice and expression grow darker.

"Well, I've got papers for you, but not the ones you would like to receive. You see, I've got a better offer elsewhere, and if you can't pay me thrice what they offered, then I shall see to it that you will never leave this station, at least not inside your ship."

Bjorn stares at Rahu with a face made of stone.

"What do you mean," Henrik asks.

A second later two guards appear behind Rahu.

"Do not move!"

Viterin who has managed to stay hidden behind a couple of boxes hunches down to avoid being detected. Rahu's men pat Henrik and Bjorn down and handcuff them.

"Where do you want us to take them?"

"Bring them to the airlock. Let's see how much we can squeeze out of them."

Viterin carefully follows them closely, hunching behind boxes along the way.

They stop next to one of the old air vents, which looks like it hasn't been used in ages. The guards stand relatively relaxed now that they see that Henrik and Bjorn are not doing anything to fight back. They are armed, but Viterin takes his opportunity and shoots one of the guards in his legs with the pulse gun set on stun. He falls on the floor and Rahu's expression shows how greatly he is surprised by Viterin's appearance. The other guard backs down.

"Put down your weapons, gentlemen," Viterin shouts. "Guard, release Bjorn and Henrik, move slowly. One bad move and I pull the trigger."

When Henrik and Bjorn are released, Viterin hand-cuffs the guard and Rahu. Viterin almost hears Rahu's heartbeat stop when he realizes that this was a big, failed attempt.

"Now, tell us why you betrayed us! And who did you betray us for?"

Rahu faces the floor and exhales loudly. His beard looks disfigured.

"It was a bluff, believe it or not. I needed the money, but now I only feel humiliated. Let me show you the proof; in my left jacket pocket you will see a sheet with all the information you need."

Viterin finds it and gives it to Bjorn.

"This contains the address for your details. Add it to your ship's identity. It's secured and verified to the ledger, now leave."

"Know that you are only spared because it's the most human thing to do," Bjorn says as they start to leave the traitor behind.

When they have walked a bit, they suddenly hear the slamming sound of an airlock door as it closes.

"That was an airlock, I'm sure of it! Let's get

back and check it out."

As they reach the area again, they see that Rahu has managed to free himself and is standing in the airlock, looking straight at them with empty eyes.

"No, wait," Henrik shouts, but it's too late. Rahu presses the button and vanishes into the dark, cold space outside.

Part 17, One Step Closer

H enrik is relieved when he sees Joanna standing near the gate. He walks to her and holds his arms tight against her in a warm embrace, sensing the sweet scent of her hair rushing into his nostrils.

"My love. I hope that you didn't have to wait long for us."

She just shakes her head and smiles.

"Just got here, sweetheart. We thought that you would be standing here, waiting for us when we arrived, but it looked like we both got occupied in something more time consuming than we thought at first."

Henrik raises his eyebrows and just nods for a while, taking in her beauty before he continues.

"So, what did you two get involved in, my love?"

"It was a bit frustrating and heart-breaking but perhaps I should let Sofie explain. It was she who needed the help, she's been through a lot this day."

Sofie hugs her dad and starts to explain what has happened. When she is done, she says, "I will stay here on Odyssey for a while. I have accommodations that our new friend Hudseon has prepared for me, I will come to Zuood as soon as possible to join you."

Bjorn looks with the concerned eyes of a father at Sofie, reflecting over what he should say for a second or two.

"I understand that you feel the need to make sure that justice is served and that your late friend Gox was very important to you. I will send over one of our guards to aid you and hope that you will be able to leave this place soon."

Sofie hugs Bjorn again and they say goodbye.

Once back in the shuttle Henrik says, "A good shower, some fresh clothes and dinner, that's what I see when I close my eyes now."

Bjorn chuckles softly, Joanna leans back and against Henrik's shoulders.

"Let's get back to our ship now."

The man in the control room gives them a clearing to leave the station. After a few seconds the bay is depressurized and the doors are opening, Bjorn starts the shuttle and exits the bay.

When they are out, he contacts Viterin, who is in the other shuttle.

"Viterin, when you get back to Eclipse, find the best guard we have and assign him to Sofie as her private bodyguard and escort him to the station. I wouldn't let my only child go unprotected in there for a longer time than necessary, especially now when she is on such a dangerous mission."

"I know exactly who should get the assignment, captain, a man who time after time makes me proud to have in our crew. Tate or 'the protector', as he is known, is our best and finest," Viterin answers.

"Good, I'm aware of his reputation. He is a good choice for this mission, get back to me when you have returned after escorting him down. We need to sit down and discuss how to implement our plan."

"Yes captain, see you soon"

The rest of the short trip is spent in silence, as they are all quite tired after spending several hours at the station.

Once they are back on *Eclipse*, they move up to the bridge. Henrik and Joanna want to be there when they make contact with Zuood, even if it's only a control centre they will contact. They both want to hear the voice from someone who is living and breathing on their new home world.

The mood on the bridge is relaxed, Bjorn has sent

most of the crew to take care of their belongings and to prepare the supply and equipment needed when building up their base on the ground. Bjorn seats himself down on the captain's chair and adds the address he got from Rahu into the ship's logs, making sure to double-check everything against the ledger before he contacts Zuoods Orbital Border Control. When he is done, he opens up the channel to report.

"This is Captain Bjorn on the trade vessel *Eclipse* with crew. Requests permissions to begin the approach to Zuood orbit, signing transaction now, over."

A few minutes later they receive a reply.

"This is Zuoods Orbital Border Control. The transaction is confirmed, *Eclipse*. Begin approach and immediately report when you're in orbit, then await further orders."

Bjorn turns around to talk to Henrik

"This will be a short trip, but Zuood is still too far away for us to just travel without the hyperdrive. During this final phase, we need to discuss our plan, Henrik."

"I understand. Let's take the ship into hyper-space and prepare our personal belongings first, then we'll sit down." Bjorn nods and begins to fire up the hyperdrive once again.

Henrik turns his attention over to Joanna, taking

her hand into his.

"Quite soon we will set our feet down on a completely different planet together my love. Let's go to our quarter and prepare everything we need to take with us after a nice and refreshing shower."

"It's like you can read my mind, sweetheart. This has been an intense day so far."

They begin to move away from the bridge.

"See you in the dining room later, Bjorn. We all need to eat something."

Bjorn smiles and blows some air out through his nostrils in amusement.

"I haven't even thought about food until now, my friend. See you soon."

A while later they all meet up. Bjorn and Viterin have been sitting there for some time and have plates in front of them that were once filled with food.

"We have come this far now. Let's finish it so we can get the crew involved," Henrik begins.

"Where did we stop last time? I think that we were going through the current government's system of surveillance. I believe that in order to awaken and unite the AA, we first need to find a way to get their attention and to show them that Chronos is vulnerable," Bjorn comments, looking at both Henrik and Viterin for confirmation before he continues. "Should we go through the plan from start again?"

Henrik has taken his time to get into his role, and he knows the plan like the back of his hand by now, so he starts from the top, saying, "Sounds like a good idea. Our first task before we can re-establish AA power is to find a suitable location to use as our HQ. It needs to be well hidden since we don't want Chronos to find out that we have arrived just yet. Second, we need to establish contact with the old AA members and regain their trust by sabotaging the surveillance system, but before that, we will send our best agents to infiltrate the government building and report Tidus movements."

Henrik looks at his fellow

"When we have succeeded in all of these areas then we can begin to truly challenge Chronos and to untie the people from Tidus firm grip."

Bjorn breathes in and positions his hand on Henrik's left shoulder before he gently breathes out as he lifts his brows, his voice is filled with pride as he starts to speak

"You will represent the future and be the figure of hope to the people, are you ready for this?"

Henrik sees just how proud Bjorn is, he said.

"I might never have been in a situation like this before, but with you and our competent crew at our side I am ready!" Henrik answers filled with confidence.

They are all standing on the bridge, looking anticipatingly on the view of the rhythmic visual of the hyperspace out through the window, as it suddenly shifts in the blink of an eye to present the view over a big blue planet in front of them in the distance, Henrik and Joanna breathe out when they see Zuood.

The first thing they see is that one of the planets moons have been completely occupied and altered into a humongous station, it is surrounded by ships ranging from small cargo ships to huge destroyers and everything in between.

"It has definitely changed since I was last here, this station wasn't here the last time we were in the neighbourhood," Bjorn said to Viterin without trying to hide his surprise, Viterin only nods as an answer.

Viterin points towards the side of the moon

"Can you all see the shipbuilding platform they have connected to the moon station?"

"Yeah, what about it?" Henrik curiously asks.

"Don't you see that the ship that is being built is of the same model as the Man of war ship that we encountered before? let me show you on the holo screen."

Henrik and Bjorn turn around and face the holo screen, what they see is most definitely the same model if not the same ship as it is being built.

"How long does it take to build a ship of that size?" Henrik said.

"It depends on many variations, but I would say around ten years more or less, I believe that this ship is a predecessor to the one we found and there might be more that is being built on different locations."

They are slowly moving into a closer orbit before they report to Z.O.B.C, Bjorn is careful to not do anything that would be out of the ordinary for a cargo crew, like going too close or staying too far away and not reporting their arrival.

"This is captain Bjorn on trade ship Eclipse, reporting arrival to Zuood orbit."

"This is Zuoods Orbital Border Control, your arrival is noted, state your purpose of visit?"

Bjorn straightens his shoulders and answers confidently.

"We are here to conduct trade with local partners, we need permission to land two shuttles near Kionidoo."

"Permission granted, your shuttles need to complete the scanning procedures on the station before entering Zuood airspace. After an approved scan you are free to land."

"Affirmative."

Part 18, Arrival

A short time after they were cleared from the security scanning on the moon station, the two shuttles began their approach towards Zuood. This time they have filled the shuttles with *Eclipse*'s finest and most well-suited crew members for the first preparations of their new headquarters. Henrik, Bjorn, and Joanna, together with five others, have begun their final approach towards the atmosphere.

Bjorn, who is sitting in the pilot seat, rotates his head so that he is facing Henrik. His smile is filled with anticipation, as he has longed for their return to Zuood. Henrik answers his smile with a nod that is meant to convey that he is prepared and ready for the task at hand, after they are both satisfied with their silent conversation Bjorn picks up the radio and contacts Viterin.

"Bjorn to shuttle two, can you hear me, Viterin?"

A few seconds go by.

"Loud and clear, Captain. What's on your mind?"

"Just to make the last adjustment on your landing coordinates, you are to fly to a nearby town of your choice, and when you and the crew arrive, I want you to stay low for a few days. Prepare a secondary base that we can use if necessary, you know the drill."

"That is wise, but wouldn't they notice that I go outside the zone that we have a permit to move around in? They definitely will notice our landing, won't they?"

"Don't worry about that. Davood gave me something that will cover your movement and trick their Ladar and heat-tracking systems into thinking that you are still on the same trajectory as me, just a few hundred meters behind all the time."

"Ok then, let me know as soon as I can change my route."

Bjorn once again shifts his attention over to Henrik.

"Now we just need to touch down in a secure area in the outskirts of...Kionidoo." His tone shifts over to a low and drawn-out pronunciation of the town and his brows have taken a sharper form, as if what he just said had triggered an instinctive thought and concern. "When we have established our base of operations, my friend, our main objective should be to build our strength, and we need to be cautious. Even though the people of Zuood are controlled by fear and forced labour, there is a group of individuals, elites of their class, that is loyal until death to their leader Tidus. They will stop at nothing if they find out that we have arrived."

Henrik sees the seriousness in Bjorn's face.

"I suppose that is the reason that you want Viterin and the others to travel to a different location first before they join us, as an extra measure of security."

"You are correct, my friend."

The shuttle touches the atmosphere. Even with the dampeners on full strength this has become a bumpy ride. Henrik gazes, wide-eyed with fascination, out the front window.

The friction from outside ignites the atmosphere around the shuttle and all Henrik sees through the window is a warm red glow. Some small drips of something are gathering on the window, he thinks that it looks like it could be water.

"Is this normal?" Henrik asks, but no one can hear him due to the noise. It stays like this for almost a minute, then everything around them calms down. The red glow is gone and replaced with a view so magnificent that Henrik has trouble believing the authenticity of what he sees.

"Those clouds over there," he gasps before continuing, "They rain upwards!"

"It's an artificial cloud." Bjorn chuckles as he begins to explain. "Some seasons on this planet prevent natural clouds from forming in certain parts, so we take the help from these manufactured clouds to give some shade and to make sure that the ground gets all the moisture it needs. It is much more effective than traditional ways of keeping the air cool and moist. The reason for it shooting upwards is that we found it to both be more effective and look a bit artsier. If you are lucky enough to be standing in the correct spot, you can see a great rainbow on top of the cloud with the base on each side of the cloud. It's a great sight."

They descend further, going on a route that will partly cover their movements and partly give Joanna and Henrik an overview of their new home planet. They soar over the landscape, seeing beautiful hills and rivers in the valleys. Some kind of animal, similar to a deer, Henrik believes, but much larger and with a blue body, can be seen in the valley. Even though Zuood is an incredibly developed planet, its nature and forests are well-taken-care-of. Bjorn slows the shuttle down a bit, descending all the way down to the treetops, just behind a hill.

"Joanna, Henrik, I believe that you should stand

up now and come to the front with me. You will like what you see when we get over this hill in front of us."

When they are in position, Bjorn ascends over the hill and the great silhouette of Kionidoo takes up all of their view. Henrik who saw it before, when he and Bjorn used the cube, is mesmerized; the feeling of actually seeing his hometown, his origin, is almost unbelievable. He uses both of his hands to rub his eyes with his palms, as if what he is seeing isn't real and that he might just be dreaming it all. But no, he actually sees Kionidoo. The hill is even the same hill as they visited in the cube simulation.

"I hope that you like this view, my friend. This is your home, your Zuood, your Kionidoo," he says.

They fly slowly towards the city, giving Joanna and Henrik a tour of their new home, as this could be the only opportunity to do this for some time. It might be too dangerous to do it later on. As they approach street level, they see that it is filled with people rushing towards something. They see that what looked good from far away isn't so at this level. The streets are filled with dirt and garbage and the people all look down, facing the ground. The splendour and grace the city gave off from far away are replaced with a feeling of decay, a sense that something is missing and has gone terribly wrong.

"The YMG, Youllian Military Guards, and police force observe every street, every corner of the city," Bjorn explains. "The punishment for theft or disobedience is more than often brutal beatings and lifelong prison sentences. It's not often anyone dares to do anything about it, but small resistance groups are still somewhat active," Bjorn says with a dark mood on his face. "This is what we are fighting against." Henrik's face hardens when he sees the guards. His lips tighten and he wants to shout out and jump down to the street, but the shuttle turns around a corner and moves away from the centre of the town.

Once they have moved to a calmer area, the shuttle suddenly dips downwards and into a narrow alley, taking another ninety-degree turn down to a parking space below one of the buildings before it stops.

"This is one of the possible positions for our headquarters. We must check the premises and see if it suits us. It's an abandoned old warehouse. We are now on the basement floor where we would cover the entrance and set up a shop on the ground floor, to make our movements here as non-suspicious as possible."

Once they have disembarked the shuttle, they quickly unload everything; the crew unpacks equipment and swiftly arranges computers and screens to make a first command central.

"Take these cameras and place them in every corner of the above floor, we need to start making the warehouse look occupied."

Part 19, Satisfied Nakamoto

After travelling on *Eclipse* for a long time, even with the artificial gravity engaged more or less the entire time, Henrik thought that the sensation of actually standing on solid ground once more was refreshing for the legs. He sees the stairs leading up to the ground floor of the building, and with one arm filled with cameras, he walks up.

We really need to get the rest of the crew down here to help out; this facility is huge, he thinks as he leaves the stairs behind him. *It looks to have been abandoned for some time, maybe a couple of years or less. How come no one else has bothered to take over the place and establish some kind of business inside* His thought gets disrupted when he remembers the cameras in his hand. *Right let's get these mounted!* There isn't much more to see other than a lot of empty warehouse shelves and one or two boxes containing dust. He takes a stroll at this level, making sure to mount the cameras in good locations, covering the entire floor, before going back down.

Joanna, who has been helping with the unpacking, sees Henrik coming down the stairs. She moves swiftly towards him.

"How are you, my love?" she says with a bright smile as her shining, crow-black hair slowly dances when she stops next to him. Her smile makes his heart skip a beat.

"Now it's amazing. You give me hope and renewed spirit. How are you dear? How are we doing with the base?"

"You sweet man, I'm good my love" she says. "The makeshift control room is starting to take shape now. I'm greatly impressed but not surprised in the swift and well-organized way they had prepared everything. All the monitors and computers, boxes with food and supplies; we have even started to work on getting an area functioning as a common dining area. I'm so impressed with our team, dear," she says.

"Glad to hear that you sound optimistic about our endeavour. I've been thinking, I want you to be in charge of the R.T.T, the Responsible Task Team. You will be amazing at that."

"The Responsible Task Team?" she curiously asks.

"Your mission is to give advice and follow the

voice of the people, making sure that we are on track with the people and continue to be favoured. Your biggest task will be to secure and prevent any smear and dirty tricks from Chronos when they begin to come for us in a not-so-distant future," Henrik explains.

"I see, that makes sense," she says. "I will begin the preparations immediately, so we have a team ready for the task as soon as possible, love." Joanna gives him one last seductive smile as she begins to walk over to the control desk. Henrik takes a deep breath as he watches her and lets it out in an equally deep exhale. Henrik's thoughts are interrupted as Bjorn suddenly stands next to him, by the look on him he is in a great and cheerful mood, unconsciously, he holds out his hands with his palms outwards in a wide arch to show with his entire body that he has something very interesting to say.

"My friend, we have been in contact with one of the old AA generals, Roukia, who is still loyal to the cause. We will meet her later today when we move out to the Kio Square, but first let's discuss something else."

"Great news, what is it that you want to talk about, my friend?"

"I have heard some rumours regarding an anomaly in the asteroid belts in the outskirts of the solar system, something about asteroids that have begun to move of their own accord, very interesting."

"Asteroids that move by themselves, that's a new one, but what about it right now? What can we do today? I want to explore it, but how should we?"

"No need for us to do anything about it right now, but I found it very interesting, I've sent a shuttle out to report their sightings."

Henrik nods to show his approval.

"Now let's gather everyone and get a well-deserved lunch break before we meet up with Roukia."

Bjorn places two of his fingers in a V-shape between his lips and whistles loudly to get everyone's attention.

"Lunch break everyone, to celebrate that we finally have arrived at Zuood. There is a feast prepared, not that extravagant, perhaps, but it's something."

Near the shuttle, Henrik sees two large containers. He opens one of them and finds a selection of different meats and two fragrant stews. In the other container they find beverages, fine wine, and some kind of dessert. Henrik sits down beside a heavily built man named Serge, whom he recently became acquainted with; he is a resourceful man with an energy that makes it easy to befriend him.

Serge is also known to have a deep, guttural voice that echoes respect, but at the same time he always talks with a gentle touch on his tongue even when he is noticeably upset and agitated. It sometimes can make people feel oddly confused, but mostly comfortable.

"What's your opinion on our location, Serge?" Henrik asks as he takes a spoonful of the hot and tasty stew.

"It is as good as any facility, I suppose. We are quite close to the false government house" he clenches his fist and slowly said, "damn those bastards . . ."

"And we have a good start point for our operation, when we are finished with setting up the mock factory upstairs, we are good to go."

"I hear, I find this place fitting as well, we only have one problem that I believe that you can help me with Serge, could you?

"Whatever you need, I will find a way."

"Good. I need you to prepare as many exit points as possible from this basement. One of them should preferably be a hidden tunnel that leads to an adjacent building that can act as a last line of defence in case we need to swiftly get out of here."

"I will make that happen, sir. One suggestion... when we get reinforcement from *Eclipse*, we let one of the shuttles be hidden and ready at the adjacent building so that we can jump away with it if it gets really nasty."

"Great idea, Serge, I trust you on this." Henrik finishes his stew, stands up, and gives Serge a friendly pat on the shoulder before he gathers desserts for both of them. Joanna, who's been sitting with her new team, comes over.

"Hello gentleman, this lunch was most satisfactory, but what is this dessert called? It's delicious," she says with delight and happiness in her eyes.

"It's a local dessert called Dejou, a sort of cheesecake, you might say. We often eat it when there is something to celebrate," Serge explains before he eats the whole thing at once.

"It really is a great-tasting dessert. I'm loving it." Her mouth forms a wide and happy smile as she locks eyes with Henrik.

A couple of minutes later Bjorn reminds Henrik that it is time to leave for the meeting with Roukia.

"Let's get going, my friend. Time waits for no one," he says excitedly. He has changed his outfit to a black polo shirt in an effort to better blend in, Henrik notices. He kisses Joanna and leaves together with Bjorn. They move rapidly out of the building, taking a pulse gun with them before they leave, just in case.

"How will we travel to the city square and locate

Roukia?" Henrik asks.

"That's the easy part, my friend. Despite Kion-idoo being controlled through fear, the ease of transportation is simply astonishing. We already have a transport waiting for us around the next corner."

"Great, and do you know the whereabouts of Roukia?"

"Of course, I do, my friend! She is waiting for us inside the Satisfied Nakamoto, one of the few authentic bistros that are left in Kionidoo. They serve the most delicious food you can imagine, one of my favourites," Bjorn answers before they arrive at a dark grey transportation pod that will take them to the square. The outer shape of the pod is built very narrow with two seats, one seat in front of the other, like in a cockpit of a fighter jet, Henrik notices that it is balancing on two partly-hidden wheels.

"The pod contains a gyro that stabilizes it, and the aerodynamic design makes it very energy ef-ficient," Bjorn briefly explains. The pod begins to travel autonomously as soon as they both are seated. The ride is short and after a few minutes, they arrive at the square.

As he leaves the vehicle, the first thing Henrik notices is the remarkable resemblance the Kio Square has with every other square he experienced on Earth.

"Exactly the same old feeling when entering a square as you would expect to feel at any. The only difference I see is the non-existent road," he says as they look around and see all the differently-lit, ground-floor shops all around the square and how they struggle to fit between the various restaurants and bars.

"Take the lead, my friend," Henrik says as they leave the pod behind them.

Bjorn quickly locates the bistro, which is easy to spot as there's a large sign that rises vertically from the corner in front of them. With fast pace and determination, they reach the entrance in couple of minutes. Once inside, Bjorn sees Roukia sitting in one of the booths at the rear wall. She has become quite elderly by now, but by the look of it she could still give a hell of a punch if the need for it came.

Bjorn waits until she notices him, then he gives her a small sign to trust them by holding his hands together in front of him, forming the shape of an arrowhead with his fingers and thumbs.

"Remember this sign, my friend; it will be useful in the future," Bjorn whispers to Henrik as they slowly approach the booth. As they come closer, Henrik notices how her eyes are cold and calculating towards them.

"Welcome to Kionidoo, my friends. I hope that

you aren't hungry. I've already eaten, but please order a drink so we don't just sit here looking awkward," she says without a smile.

"Thank you, General," Henrik says.

"No need to be that formal, Henrik, Heir of Andromeda. I want to get straight to the point of our meeting, if that is ok for you. I have a couple of questions for you and I have limited time," she quickly replies.

"That is of no problem for us, Roukia. Ask your questions and I will answer as best as I can."

"How come you weren't informed from when you were young about your position and role in Zuood? I'm aware that you have lived for the most part on a different planet, so how can we trust that your understanding and knowledge of how to rule is up to the standards that it must be met in our society?" she begins.

"I understand your concern and doubt, but I must ask you to understand something about me. During my entire life I've had a feeling in the back of my head that something was missing, and now I've found it. My new mission in life is to restore the peace and prosperity of my people," Henrik replied.

"So you say, Henrik, but how will you prove it for the rest of us?" she remarks.

Bjorn tries to get into the conversation. "Roukia, are you familiar with the Madreaki test? Let Henrik

152

undergo it and let there be no doubt in the future. We can assess his quality most efficiently and effectively this way."

"Madreaki test?" Henrik wonders silently.

"I'm familiar with it. I believe we have all the necessary equipment to perform such a test in our camp," Roukia answers with a slightly questioning look on her face. "And I do believe in its worth as a way to assess the ability of a leader."

"What is this so-called Madreaki test that you two talk about?"

"It's quite simple, my friend. You will be faced with different tasks in a VR environment that will challenge your ability to make swift decisions and test your judgement. Your actions will be performed through your thoughts. You will have sensors connected on your neck and forehead, and the visual will be given to you through a similar cube that you have used before," Bjorn explains.

"I understand, sounds simple enough," Henrik replies.

"Don't be fooled. It isn't as easy as you might believe, no matter who you are, and no matter what kind of person you think you are," Roukia remarks, her voice dry and harsh.

Henrik raises his brows before he says, "What are we waiting for? Let's prepare for my test."

Part 20, Integrity, and hard choices

T hey are gathered in one of Roukia's safe-houses, located on the outskirts of Kionidoo. Before they arrived, Roukia sent a request to other members of the old AA to join as spectators of this test. Bjorn and Roukia prepare the test environment for Henrik, going through the last adjustments and checking the source code for any parameters that need to be adjusted to better suit Henrik's physiology. When they are sure that everything is correct, Bjorn turns his attention to Henrik and explains that the test will be done in a chamber separated from the rest of the safehouse. For the test to be verifiable and the results undeniable, the procedure needs to be done in a controlled environment. A couple of members have now joined, veterans of old and new blood, with stern and curious eyes they look upon Henrik as he stands beside Roukia.

"It's up to you now, Henrik to prove your worth. If you succeed, then I and the other members will support you and begin the work to rebuild the old AA network and spread the word of your mission. Let's waste no time; let the test begin," Roukia says with a smile that Henrik thinks can be interpreted as mischievous and false, but quickly casts away that notion and focuses his energy towards the task at hand.

Henrik enters the test chamber and grabs the prepared cube; with a gentle touch he triggers it to start the simulation. The simulation environment is at first almost empty of details, almost sterile. He finds himself standing in a room that is somewhat similar in the way it is constructed to his living room back on Earth. He sees the couch and simple pixelated resemblance of plants. All the colours are off from what he expects them to be; the room is grey and dull. Bjorn's friendly and focused voice is heard in the background.

"The environment you are in now my friend is different for everyone. It's drawn from your own mind and will evolve and transform around you depending on the choices you make from the challenges you will face. Try to focus on an object you see and change it."

Henrik looks around in the room and his eyes close in on one of the plants in the corner in front of him. He stares at it and focuses his will. After a while, he gets the hang of it and succeeds with his wish to change to plant into a lamp, a simple practice task, he figured. Now it's time to pick up the pace. He wanders around the room, getting a feeling of the environment and what actions he can do and what he cannot change, testing the boundaries of the code. As he moves around the room, changes and more details are added from every footstep he makes; the rendering of the environment gets updated in real-time.

"This reminds me a lot of the same interactive-ability that I have witnessed in VR games back on earth, except the graphics are undeniably perfect. I see no difference to this compared to what can be seen outside this virtual environment. I will proceed forward now and leave my old living room," Henrik said with an excited voice as he moves towards the next area.

As he leaves the room, he enters an area that shares no resemblance to his old living room or house. The new environment tastes like iron and sulphur on his tongue. He is outside in some kind of wildlands, and on the horizon over the treetops, he sees the disturbing sight of a green moon. It shines sinisterly as Henrik turns his head around in fast and searching movements, trying to get his directions in order. He is surrounded by a forest; the trees look primaeval as they stretch far into the sky. On top of a hill, he sees an old mansion with dark ivy growing on all sides of the building, only letting small sections of windows be visible to the naked eye. Henrik moves towards it.

"I don't know what my mind is up to or what kind of test this is, but I'll soon find out I guess," he says to himself, almost as a reply to someone's question.

As he closes in on the mansion, something catches his eye: a broad staircase leading to the entrance of the building, the only light that is emitted from the house comes from a lonely window on the top floor of the mansion.

"Someone or something is inside the building in front of me. This must be the beginning of the first test...I'm going inside," he says to let the spectators know his intentions and his dedication as he proceeds up the stairs. Henrik reaches toward the large door handle that greets him, slowly opening the massive door by pulling it towards him.

"Wait, what is this?" Henrik gasps as he is sucked in through the opening, the door slamming shut behind him.

On the other side, the environment is completely transformed. He is back on the *Eclipse*, standing in the lower corridor leading to the engine room. Emergency lights are flashing rapidly in the corridor with the same sinister nuance of green as the moon before.

"I'm back at *Eclipse*, down low, proceeding with caution," Henrik says as he moves through the corridor.

"I see some kind of slimy substance on the walls and the floor. I will stay away from it just in case," Henrik mentions to the spectators. He walks in a slow and focused manner towards the engine room, taking mental notes of everything in front of him. In the air, he can feel the presence of someone. *I'm not alone in here...whoever you are or whatever you might be, I will prevail.* Henrik opens the door, visually inspecting the room before entering. The inside of the room looks somewhat as it should, with no indication of anything like in the corridor he now stands in. As he enters, he is met by the robot Mary, greeting him with a slowly buzzing noise of malfunctioning electronic and a very disfigured metal body. Henrik can see that cables have been ripped from the arms. The air is thickened by the smoky odour of fried circuits. After a short while, he determines that Mary isn't of more interest for the test, so he moves on, past the robot, and further into the engine room, entering the engine compartment zone.

"The engines are not engaged. I see no further signs of anything unusual in here. It is spot-on as it should be, except one thing," he reports to the outside, making sure that they know that he hasn't forgotten that this is a test and that they will give remarks on his every action, testing his limits. He moves alongside one of the large engines, slowly putting his left hand on the mechanics and whistling to himself. Henrik is certain now that he isn't alone in the room; someone is lurking in the corner, ready to strike. As he reaches the end of the engine he stops, takes a breath and without any hesitation swiftly rotates his body 180 degrees, so as he faces the side he came from.

His eyes meet the horrifyingly greyish and cold face of Loukh, who has been brought back to life. He is now much taller than he was as a living person. Their gazes are locked to each other. Henrik twists in agony as Loukh pierces into Henrik's eyes and it feels like a blade is going through his brain as a nauseating headache grips the very existence of Henrik's world into its force. He can hear Moktai's agonizing voice whispering his need for help as Loukh grabs onto Henrik's shoulder before vanishing into thin air. Henrik does his best not to fall on his knees and lose the last little control over his body that he still has. He can still feel the chillingly cold touch on his shoulder.

When the pain slowly releases its grip, a single word is stuck in Henrik's mind on repeat: *Airlock,*

airlock.... He feels forced to obey the thought, so Henrik begins to move at a fast pace towards the nearest airlock he knows. He rushes out from the engine compartment, past Mary, and up the stairs to the living areas. Continuing past Loukh's old quarters, he hears the faint sound of someone saying *traitor*. Henrik ignores this and quickens his pace.

"I need to reach the airlock before it's too late," he shouts while at the same time feeling confused about what will happen when he arrives. *Too late for what?* He does not know what to expect. The corridor narrows in on him as he closes in on a passageway leading to one of the airlocks on the starboard side of the quarterdeck. He feels faint and weakened as he once again faces the cold eyes of Loukh through the small round airlock porthole, standing with a straight back and with his arms pointed straight down. His face is completely emotionless.

"What do you want, what is my task?" Henrik begins to ask the pale figure inside. No answer.

Henrik notices that a countdown clock is positioned in front of Loukh. It begins to count down from one hundred. As he gathers his thoughts, a panel opens on the airlock hatch with two buttons, two choices: *Open* or *Pardon.* Henrik quickly considers the options and with a determined motion he presses *Pardon.* At first, nothing happens, but a second later the inside hatch opens, Henrik notices that Loukh's appearance has drastically changed, from the pale and grim-looking figure from before, he now looks as he did when he was alive.

"Thank you," he says as he slowly fades out of sight.

Part 21, Unexpected company!

The airlock area is once again calm and no sounds are heard as Henrik releases the tension that he built up in his body. He lets out a deep breath of air, regaining his focus. He is still facing the open airlock hatch, but the buttons have disappeared. The sight of Loukh's body returning to normal state had felt calming and satisfying; the atmosphere in the room was quiet.

"That was something else, wasn't it?" he says with a low voice as he turns around, walks out of the room, leaving the airlock, feeling satisfied with his efforts in this test.

He walks along the corridor, once again past Loukh's quarters. The emergency lights are turned off and the entire ship feels empty of life, of energy itself. Henrik decides to inspect the bridge, uncertain of what the purpose might be but that is what feels like the right thing to do next. The walk up is slow, on the way he passes his and Joanna's quarters. *If I only could have you by my side now,*

you always make everything so much easier my love.
forgetting that almost everything is possible in this
environment.

As Henrik walks out from the corridor and
into the bridge, the air is filled with voices
from crewmembers discussing different objects,
controlling outer and inner statuses of the ship
on bright displays. The entire bridge is buzzing
with energy. Henrik notices that something has
happened in here, some sort of conflict. Parts of the
bridge are destroyed and uncountable fragments
of wooden shrapnel from exploded crates are all
around the huge bridge area. Henrik smiles as he
sees Joanna and Bjorn standing furthest out on the
bridge, inspecting and moving at a fast pace around
the holographic screen that visualizes some sort
of huge man-built construction. They seem to be
highly engaged in a discussion of some sort, Henrik
notices as he closes in on them; they haven't seen
him yet.

"We need to move immediately, do all that it
takes to return the artefact to our possession. Without it we can't complete the process, we will be
stuck here in the absolute void of space." Joanna's
voice is calm and controlled; she has always been a
born leader.

"I am aware of that, my dear, a shuttle is being
prepared as we speak," Bjorn answers.

They both turn around to greet Henrik.

"Glad that you are here, my friend. We need to move out quickly. As you are aware the creature took the artefact and escaped down to the asteroid base by hijacking one of the escape pods, give us the order and we move immediately," Bjorn says.

"What creature are you two talking about? I'm sorry, but I didn't see it up close unfortunately," Henrik asks.

"What do you mean, my friend, you were the one that first sounded the alarm before it attacked!" Bjorn answers, sounding a bit perplexed.

"Anyway," he continues, "It is unlike any other living thing we have come across on our journey so far, fast as a tachyon and eerily dark as the inside of a tube, almost as if it was made of smoke. It didn't even bother to kill, it just threw things around as if they were made of feathers. When it found the ancient artefact, it disappeared as quickly as it had attacked, and you are telling me that you didn't even see it. My friend, I'm telling you, this is something else." Bjorn looks away and around the bridge.

Joanna hands Henrik a pulse gun that he swiftly holsters.

"No doubt that it was fast, but maybe Bjorn exaggerates it just a little bit. Let's move out and reclaim the artefact, my love. We need to find the strength and courage to do all that is required from us, we can do it together." Her voice is just as sweet in Henrik's ears as it always is.

"I will always do my best for you, my love," Henrik answers as he drowns in her eyes.

"Hrm hrm," Bjorn interrupts, "lovebirds, we need to go now," he says as he begins to move down the bridge and towards the nearest exit. Henrik and Joanna follow.

Once they reach the shuttle, Bjorn hands over a protective suit, completely black except for yellow stripes that go parallel from the helmet and down towards the boots.

"Suit up. We believe that the auto-defence system is operative on the base. We will not be able to land on the asteroid, so we need to use the existing gravity field to make a jump from our shuttle and hopefully land on the steel platform below," Bjorn says as he too changes to the same kind of outfit, the only difference being that the stripes on his suit are red.

As soon as Henrik sits down, the shuttle begins to move. With a swooshing sound, the craft passes the shield of *Eclipse* and a trajectory is plotted towards the asteroid base. They quickly arrive above the base, which looks dead as no other lights are seen other than some sort of rotating lights positioned on top of antenna-like structures. They shine in the same sinister green shade as Henrik has seen previously.

"Time to jump. All ready and set?" Henrik takes command and asks the handful of crewmembers inside the shuttle, including Joanna and Bjorn. The shuttle closes in as near as possible, around four hundred meters away from the platform. They must fall controlled and hopefully land on their feet. The shuttle hatch opens. As Henrik takes one step outside, he is stopped by Bjorn's strong grip.

"What if this doesn't work, my friend?"

"Don't worry, it will work, trust me," Henrik answers and takes the leap out from the shuttle, headfirst towards the surface of the asteroid. The fall isn't as rapid as Henrik first thought it would be—the gravitational force from this far out isn't strong enough to pull them fast towards the surface—so the fall is more of a careful descent. As Henrik falls, he makes small adjustments on his trajectory with the suit's built-in minimal nozzle thrusters, making sure that he aligns himself with the rest of the group.

Halfway on the trip, he rotates his head and body so that he can see if the others are in correct positions; they are all synchronized in the descent. *This goes quite smoothly right now. I wonder what the algorithm has in store for me*, Henrik thinks as he remembers that he still is in a virtual reality environment, even though he feels that the experience is almost impossible to distinguish from reality itself. He rotates back facing the asteroid base. He can now distinguish different details down below. The entire asteroid looks to be hollowed out and filled with passageways, both inner and outer metal gangways where parts of the railing are incomplete is built alongside the passageways. Perhaps they could be used for inspections and repairs, Henrik reasons. The sinister green lights flash rapidly around the antennas that are positioned all along the base, on almost every corner.

The velocity is greater as they get near the artificial gravity field. They are around forty meters away from the platform as Henrik curls up to a ball to begin the rotation of his body so that he falls feet first, the nozzles thrust holds him aligned with the surface. The others follow suit and do the same manoeuvre.

Where did I gain the knowledge of how to manoeuvre this type of suit? Must be some subconscious act of interplay with the algorithm powering this simulation, Henrik silently concludes. He adds, *To simplify and enhance the experience, I suppose* to complete his own thought.

Thrusters located in the boots explode into full power as they reach the last meter before landing on the surface. A few seconds later they are all standing on the dark and cold base.

"Let's set up parameters somewhere along the way. The creature is somewhere on this base," Henrik says as he looks across one of the passageways going straight towards the middle of the base. There is no sign indicating that they aren't alone on this abandoned base.

Part 22, The Creature!

The group begins to move towards one of the passageways leading straight towards the centre of the asteroid. The artificial gravity field holds them firmly on the surface, but as a precaution, Henrik has told them all to keep their mag-boots ready, just in case.

"Did any of you spot the escape pod? Was it on the surface?" Henrik asks as he reaches out and grabs the railing on his right side, turning his head and body around so that he can see the group.

"No signs as far as I can tell at least. Perhaps the creature ditched it on the other side of the aster-oid?" Joanna says as she too grabs a firm grip on the railing. Bjorn and the other crewmembers agree that that must be the case. None one identified a pod on their way down. Henrik returns his gaze towards the passageway once again, going over the idea he has in his head regarding how to achieve this task of returning the artefact.

"The first thing to do should be to get the creature out of hiding. The next action we should take must be to somehow paralyze the creature so that we can catch it," Henrik says as they reach the first passageway. "Now let's get inside this tube and see if we can find anything interesting,"

Henrik takes a firm grip on a handle on the side of the metal wall, pulls the handle down, and opens the hatch. The other follow through to the inside. It's dark in here; not even the sinister green lights are seen anymore. Henrik proceeds to activate the four strong headlights positioned on the upper part of the suit's helmet.

"Now we can see what we will face in here, let's go," Henrik casually says before he moves further in, making sure that the rest of the crew is behind him. The passageway is quite narrow on the inside, making it difficult to move along. The floor is cluttered with damaged cables, fallen boxes, and old, almost random things that look to be out of context in this environment. As they move further and further in, a buzzing sound is heard faintly in the background, but as they get closer to the source the sound fills up more and more of the surrounding.

"Stay cautious, my love, don't rush it to the end," Joanna whispers in a private channel to Henrik.

"I will my dear."

As they reach a sharp right turn in the passageway, Henrik sees that it leads to an entire room inside the base. The only problem is that they are all just standing on a platform out in the air. They can see nothing except the platform that is lit with the sinister green light as seen before and a railing going down to a ladder. They are well above the floor, they all conclude as they can't see the bottom.

"Throw down a flare," Henrik orders. Bjorn takes out a flare from his suit, twists the top to ignite it, and throws it down the platform. The bright, red light twists and turns on the way down, becoming fainter and fainter until it can no longer be seen.

"That isn't a good sign my friend, what's your order, sir?" Bjorn asks before he continues, "The buzzing sound is most definitely coming from somewhere down the room, we must act."

Henrik takes a moment to decide and then with a ladder as the only way down, begins to take slow steps, holding the railing and making sure that it will hold.

"Move down. Make sure to keep some distance to each other to even out the weight. We can't be sure that the ladder will hold, stay safe and don't use the thrusters if it isn't absolutely necessary. We don't want to warn the creature if it is down there somewhere," Henrik says as he takes a firm but gentle enough grip on both sides of the ladder and begins to glide down.

Almost ten meters at a time is all that he dares to glide before making a stop, inspecting the ladder down to make sure that it will continue, time and time again he does this. His arms are beginning to feel weary by now and as Henrik begins to wonder if they will ever reach the bottom, he starts to notice the faint light from the flare again.

"Soon down, be careful," Henrik reports up the ladder.

A few minutes later, they are all standing on firm ground again, the room looks to be a hollow part of the asteroid as rock formations are formed all around them.

"Let's continue forward my brave crew, I bet that the creature is lurking somewhere in here." The light from their helmets sweeps the area as they slowly make their move further and further into the room.

The trail that they follow leads them exclusively in one direction. They are surrounded by several meters of a rock wall, making it impossible to see where exactly they are heading.

Suddenly Henrik sees the creature in front of them; it's just standing still near some sort of huge device surrounded by old railings that secures the area from a huge hole in the ground. Holding the artefact with what might be a hand, the body of the creature shifts as if it is out of sync with the simulation or something, Henrik notices.

"I know what we have to do now," Henrik says. He pulls up the pulse gun and carefully aims at the device next to the creature, hoping that it will short circuit and with a huge amount of luck. A charge will hit the creature, making it not only out of sync but maybe out entirely.

A short but precise burst from the pulse gun fills the room with a sharp light. Henrik hits the device, nothing happens.

"Shit," is all that Henrik has time to say before the creature moves very fast across the room, takes hold of him, and throws him to the side while grabbing the others and knocking them towards the rock wall. Henrik rushes towards the device and grabs the artefact that the creature in his confusion left on the ground. Loud noise and bright lights are seen as Henrik fires the pulse gun directly at the creature, getting its full attention.

The creature turns around. Without any doubt, Henrik acts as fast as he can as he notices that the creature isn't as fast as it was before; something must have happened to it. He grabs what looks to be the shoulders of the creature, forcing it down on the ground. The creature is strong, very strong but Henrik uses the thrusters on his suit to gain additional strength. In the commotion, he gets a glimpse of some of the crewmembers' destroyed suits and cracked helmets. They are smashed at the wall so hard that they cannot have survived. Henrik's mind rushes with anger.

The next move he makes takes him further to the edge of the broken metal gangway surrounding the giant hole, Henrik's left foot almost loses grip on the metal surface as he fights the gigantic creature.

This is it; I will not let you win and take away all that I hodl dear.

"Time to face your destiny and final resting place," Henrik shouts as he twists his body and steps out from the broken gangway, dragging the creature with him. He can hear Joanna's loud scream from above, calling his name.

Henrik falls into oblivion in the simulation environment; he can see the dim light from the opening above from where he took the plunge. Falling deeper and deeper until everything suddenly quiets down, the sensation of falling vanishes as if the fall never occurred. Henrik's head fills with a pulsating sensation that slowly fades away before he briefly senses someone's hands on his shoulders as his consciousness leaves him, catching him as he falls from the chair and onto the floor.

Part 23, Signs of a true leader

H enrik finds himself on top of a makeshift
stretcher as he slowly regains consciousness;
his vision is blurry at first. In his head, a deafening
noise surrounds him. He can, if only very faintly,
hear several voices chattering in the background.
He finds that it's impossible to distinguish one
voice from the other. With his hands pressed
against his skull to ease the tension and kill the
noise, he tries to get up. Henrik stands on his feet
as he mumbles towards the crowd of people in front
of him.

"W...What happened?".

Yo-Kiel, an elderly man dressed in a blue robe
that conveys respect and reminds Henrik of some
sort of outfit that generals or other high-ranked
people in movies often wear, begins to answer.

"You showed us all a great deal of leadership
skills, Henrik. To be honest, you have impressed
us and frankly surprised us during this challenge.
You have gone through all of the expectations one

can have on a true leader." From his manner and smile Henrik can see that he Yo-Kiel is sincere and open with his opinion.

Bjorn continues where Yo-Kiel ended. "You demonstrated both respect and humility when you pardoned Loukh, offered him your empathy, and gave him back his dignity. Others might not have done it, my friend, just out of pure anger towards his previous actions, but you showed us all that you have integrity as a leader."

A young man, perhaps in his upper twenties hold his hand with his palms towards Henrik as if he wished to hug him begins to say.

"If there is something I can add to this assess-ment of you, it's that I find it incredible how you had the strength, courage, and true commitment towards your service as a leader when you sacri-ficed yourself by jumping down the support struc-ture taking the giant creature with you in the fall, how did you do it?" The man continues without letting Henrik answer. "Anyway, bravo, we all feel proud to call you our leader and the true heir of Andromeda. We will be by your side and do what we must to regain control of Kionidoo and in the end the whole of Andromeda."

Henrik looks around at all the new faces and newly-gained supporters, making sure to meet their eyes one by one in an effort to show his gratitude for their words and appraisal. As he meets the eyes of Roukia, he stops, and she begins to speak.

"You have demonstrated what we wanted to see, that is correct, Henrik, but I'm not entirely convinced of you yet. I will keep a sharp eye on you at all times." Roukia concludes the meeting and leaves the room without any further words spoken.

The other people in the room shrug disapprovingly in the direction Roukia left and begin to take their turn shaking Henrik's hand. They all give their pledge to only serve in the interest of the Andromeda Alliance's new leader. Henrik answers by giving his own pledge to them. He promises to do his utmost to deliver peace and prosperity, just as Bjorn has instructed him to do in case the outcome would be positive.

As they leave one by one, Bjorn, who by the look on his face is feeling excited and energetic, puts his hand on top of Henrik's shoulder in a friendly manner as he says, "What should we do next my friend? What is your plan?"

"Now that I'm finally recognized as the leader of Andromeda Alliance and our mission can continue as planned, my first and most important task should be to visit my mother Anvu. It has been in my mind for a long time now and it's way overdue."

"I understand, Henrik. I have her last known address in my system. We can see if she still lives there right away if you would like?" Bjorn responds.

"Good, but before we do that I want to return to Joanna and take her with us when we visit my mother," Henrik says with a great smile. They walk out of Roukia's safehouse and into a pod that awaits them. The journey back to the headquarters goes smoothly. Through the tinted windows he can see how his fellow Zuoodlings wander the streets, careful not to be noticed by the military guards that are scattered all over the city. He can see old and abandoned street-level offices mixed with new and small shops as they come closer to the centre of the town.

Enormous propaganda billboards can be seen on an open field through the windows on the other side of the pod. The imagery on one of the billboards displays a prison cell with bold text next to it. Henrik has practised reading Zuoodi and can read some of the text reasonably, but eventually, he turns his head to ask Bjorn what it says.

Bjorn, who has been occupied with adding the route to their separate destinations into the pod without permitting it to cache the signature of Bjorn's login, so they stay at least somewhat hidden from Chronos for now, takes a moment to briefly glance at the billboard before he answers.

"The sentence on the billboard is hard to translate directly into English, my friend. It wouldn't make much sense for you, but the underlying meaning is that if you disobey the law in any way, you will be punished hard and without mercy, so behave."

Henrik nods silently and returns his gaze towards the billboards once more, his heart beats fast and with an anger that seldom burns inside him, his thoughts are on all the people who suffer due to the pain that Tidus together with Chronos inflicts upon them.

"When the time comes, I will rain hellfire upon Tidus and his loyal group of followers who are part of keeping the system brutal, who hold the people hostage under false leadership. The best part is that Tidus won't even notice it before it's too late," Henrik says to Bjorn.

Part 24, The reunion!

As the journey proceeds, the sun slowly begins to settle below Zuood's horizon, welcoming the night shift. For the rest of the way back, Henrik contemplates in silence the challenges that are ahead of them, wondering how his mother will react when they finally meet. His thoughts circle around his head like a system of satellites orbiting a planet. Before he can find some inner peace, the pod stops on the other side of the street, in front of the headquarters.

Joanna, who has been informed by Bjorn that they would soon return, stands just outside of the building basking in the soft light coming from a streetlight above. Henrik leaves his troubled mind inside the pod as he leaves his seat. He smiles when he sees her standing there in her tight, dark-blue, low-waist jeans and a cut off crop top. She looks stunning as always. Bjorn is right behind, leaving the pod with a surprisingly graceful and swift manner that unfortunately, no one noticed.

Standing next to the pod, Henrik watches as Joanna's beautiful, black hair sways gently as a soft breeze takes hold onto it. He has always been aware that she knows how to make an entrance, even when she isn't the one who enters the room. He notices that behind her, in the shadow, another figure lurks. *Who's that?* he briefly wonders as they both begin to walk across the street and closer to home.

Suddenly Bjorn lights up and waves with his hands towards the figure in the back.

"My sweet daughter!" he shouts as he sees that it's Sofie who is lurking in the darkness, her dark green outfit camouflage her in the dark, he is fastening his pace until he holds her in his arms.

"It makes me so happy to see you again, to hold you in my arms. When did you arrive my child?"

Henrik has reached Joanna and gives her a warm embrace and kisses her sweet lips, they both smile towards Bjorn and Sofie.

"She arrived only minutes after you two left the warehouse. My love, she has been through a lot during the short time she was away. I will let her explain when she is ready for it." Joanna says with a soft voice.

Sofie looks into her father's eyes; they are filled

with joy and happiness. It saddens her a bit that what she will later tell him will make that joy disappear. She bites her lips to get rid of the concerns that she isn't ready to reveal just yet.

"It's good to see you again, Dad. I arrived a couple of hours ago. It's cold outside; let's move to a warmer place so that we can talk."

Bjorn grabs her by the shoulder as they begin to walk towards the door leading them inside the headquarters. He had heard something sad in her voice hidden between her words. Though he's not sure what it might be, he just hopes that it isn't too serious and that it is something that can be solved.

Henrik and Joanna are right behind them. As they enter the headquarter Bjorn and Sofie walks over to the makeshift food area to get something to warm up with. Henrik and Joanna set their direction towards the nearest bench; it's made as part of a meeting area where the team can discuss topics without disturbing anyone else. They both take a seat, looking each other in the eyes.

"So, now that we are a bit more alone, how did it go? I've been so curious about what you two did when you were away. Anything interesting to tell me?" Joanna asks with a heart-warming smile on her face.

"Let me tell you, my dear..." Henrik begins as he goes through their long, exhausting, and prosperous meeting with Roukia and the old AA members step by step, describing in detail how the Madreaki test was done. When he is finished, Joanna takes his hands.

"You did great, Henrik. You make me proud to know that you are my husband. What's the plan now? What will my heir do?" she says, her voice filled with pride and affection.

"Thank you, my love. I will tell you all about the plan later, but now, how about you? Anything interesting happened here while we were away?"

Joanna nods silently with a facial expression that tells Henrik that something definitely happened and that it's good.

"You know the team you wanted me to gather, the Rapid Response Team?" she says. Without letting Henrik answer, she continues, "Well, I have managed to assemble a team that I believe in, a team that will handle the task."

"That is amazing news. The team will be essential for our later success in winning the favour of the people and keeping the Chronos propaganda under control," he replies.

They sit there on the bench for a while, contemplating the difficulties of life and how they came to be leading figures of this group of resistance. Their discussion leads to other topics. Time seems to be flying at an ever-increasing speed, yet time itself seems to have stopped around them. Henrik talks vividly and rapidly about the vision he had of his mother when he used the cube for the first time. He describes how he saw her standing on the top of the hill, how her white and blue-checkered summer dress swayed in the wind and how her familiar and warming smile made him feel safe. His voice slows down a bit as he reaches the end of his vision.

"I have no other memories of my mother. All I know is that her name is Anvu and that she is alive somewhere on this planet. Bjorn has more details and soon we will finally meet again after almost my entire life." Henrik says. Joanna sees both joy and sadness at the same time in him as she realizes that he never had the opportunity to hug his mother as an adult and let her know that she is unconditionally loved.

"I'm looking forward to meeting your mother, my love. A mother's embrace can be one of the sincerest things in life. If you're lucky enough to have a loving mother, it's important to know your heritage and to give your mother the love she deserves," Joanna says. Henrik nods as a reply as her words circle inside him and lands in his heart.

Bjorn interrupts their discussion with a friendly wave as he walks to where they sit. In his left hand he holds a heavy-looking green rucksack that looks old and damaged.

"My brave friends, today has been a very long day but you can never get tired when you have the best surprise waiting as you return to base, am I right? Sofie has told me all about the events that happened as we left the station. We missed a lot I must say, never in my wildest imaginations could I have guessed that the station was infested with so much corruption and greed." Bjorn sits down next to them, tucking away the rucksack to the side of the bench as Henrik curiously asks.

"Bjorn, my friend, you can't tell us something like that and then leave out the details, what has happened? Do we need to worry about Sofie?"

Bjorn breathed a sigh of relief before answering his friend.

"Don't worry too much, my friend. She is alright now." With a deeper tone, he begins to tell the story that Sofie told to him. "Only a few days after we left the station the leader of the gang was dismissed without any further charges other than a minor fine regarding some old bar brawl. The charges against him for the murder of my daughter's friend was dropped without any prior notice." He briefly pauses before continuing, making sure to look both Henrik and Joanna in the eyes to ensure of what comes next will be worse.

"So as the charges were dropped, the leader was

once again free to do whatever he wanted. My sweet daughter told me that she was terrified. They came after her while she slept, and she was only able to escape with the help of the man Viterin assigned to guard duty," Bjorn says with a voice that only a concerned parent can produce.

Part 25, The plan!

H enrik shakes his head slowly as he listens to Bjorn describing Sofie's escape from the station and how Tate lived up to his reputation as the best of the best. Henrik places his hand on Bjorn's shoulder and says, "We are all very relieved that Sofie is safe and back under our roof. We have to give Tate our deepest gratitude and give him the Shield award for incredible achievement in duty."

Bjorn, surprised, raises his eyebrows when he hears Henrik talk about the Shield award.

"I wasn't aware that you were familiar with the different awards officers and guards in the crew can receive. My friend, you keep showing me repeatedly that you are more than fit for the role as our leader."

"Thank you, but that's only what is expected of me," Henrik answers. Bjorn accepts the fact and proceeds to inform them about the next step in their journey, to reunite Henrik with his mother, so he turns his attention over to Joanna to explain the situation.

"As Henrik probably has told you, we will reunite him with his mother Anvu. We have her location so we know where she lives, but it will not be an easy task since the latest intel we received from our field agents reveals that Anvu is being followed by two or more agents from Chronos at all times. Every step she makes is being monitored."

"I wasn't aware that she was being followed and monitored. Why didn't you tell me before my friend?" Henrik asks, quite annoyed that his friend had withheld such crucial information from him. Bjorn senses his frustration.

"My friend, I just received the information myself, I wasn't aware of it either, until very recently. I understand your frustration and I promise you that we will get her freed from her oppressors very soon," Bjorn says.

Joanna, who is both thrilled about the fact that they will get her freed and at the same time worried about Anvu's safety, asks, "How will we save her? What's the plan?"

Bjorn holds his hands in front of him, palms facing upwards and away from his body, unsure what to say as an answer to their worries. For the first time in a long time, he feels powerless. He sees that Sofie is approaching so to at least make them feel a little bit at ease, he finally says "Don't worry,

I have given the task to figure out a plan that will work to Sofie. I believe in her and she has worked with similar tasks before, she will tell us more now as she joins us."

Sofie walks at a fast pace towards them. In her hand, she holds a heavy, brown leather rucksack. Its appearance fits together well with her dark green clothes. She approaches them with a huge smile that signals only one thing: that she is bringing good news. When she reaches them, she confidentially says, "I have devised a plan together with Serge, he wants me to inform you that he is finished with the thing you requested by the way." Sofie waits a second to give Henrik a chance to answer.

"Great! I knew I could trust him with that, now tell us about the plan you two have made, we are very interested," Henrik replies, Sofie brings out a device from her rucksack that resembles the cube in size and shape and places it on the table in front of them. When she activates it, a holographic three-dimensional map over a neighbourhood appears in front of them, showing three different markers: two near each other on the outskirts of the map and one on the corner of a building in the middle.

"Our plan is simple. Through our undercover agent, we will instruct Anvu to tell her supervisors that she will travel to the city centre to do some errands. Of course, the plan is for her to escape, but she can't tell them that obviously. I have named the mission '*Operation Bird Mom*'." she pauses for a second to look them in the eyes and see if any questions pop up.

"Well, that's kind of a quirky name, but it works I guess," Bjorn says with a great amount of spirit in his voice.

Sofie continues, "You are correct, Dad. I can't help it, but I like the name. When she travels, she is always followed by two agents in a pod right behind her, so she will leave the house and enter an empty pod waiting on the street that we hacked and have under our control." She points towards the two markers on the outskirts of the map. "These two markers represent the two pods, see now as they begin to move towards the city centre." The markers begin to move around the map, circling through the streets, Anvu's pod in the lead followed by the agents. Sofie points towards a building near the third mark on the map.

"As the pods reach this point, we will do two sharp and unexpected turns into this narrow road between the buildings, two sharp right turns and Anvu's pod will reach our shuttle, represented by the third marker." She gives them another chance to ask questions.

This time Henrik believes that he spotted some–

thing in the plan, so he asks, "So far so good I believe, but what about when she reaches our pod? What will happen then? I'm sure that if they find the empty pod, they will report it right away and we will have the entire Chronos after us in a matter of minutes."

Sofie doesn't want to take the risk of exposing the entire plan in case a mole is listening to their words, so she gives him a reassuring smile before she says, "I understand your concern and hear your question, but trust me when I say that your mother will be safe and the agents following her will be no wiser. They will only notice that she is gone way later. I don't want to ruin the surprise by giving you the final detail to my plan, but I guarantee you that this will work."

Henrik takes some time to think about what she said, gazing around the room. "I believe in you, I understand that some of the details of the plan can be better to be left alone right now, you have reassured me that my mother will be safely rescued and soon we can all sit down and enjoy a healthy meal in joyful company."

"So, let's prepare the shuttle and take care of business. Early tomorrow morning we will execute the plan," she says with an impatient and excited tone. Sofie needs this rescue mission, or any mission would suffice actually, to keep her thoughts away from the drama experienced on Odyssey station. She wants to forget about it, if only for a moment.

"You're right," Henrik says to Sofie.

"You and Bjorn will begin any needed preparation of the shuttle. Early in the morning, we will go and get geared up and ready. Hopefully, we won't find any resistance in our way on our mission, but it's better to be prepared for the worst." They begin to move out of the area. Bjorn and Sofie take the short route towards the shuttle area, passing by the control centre to pick up Serge. Henrik and Joanna walk towards the armoury and sleeping area to get some well-deserved rest.

After this eventful day, they both feel like they will fall fast asleep as soon as their heads touch the soft, inviting pillows on their bed. Henrik holds Joanna gently as she rests her head on his chest. As he draws long deep breaths his nose is filled with the sweet scent from her hair. Joanna's right hand follows the rhythm up and down as Henrik inhales and exhales.

They wake up early in the morning and it doesn't take long until they are both prepared and ready for the rescue mission. Henrik has put on a pair of highly sophisticated, low-weight running shoes with built-in dampening that he received as a gift from Bjorn as an early welcome home gift when they were still on Eclipse. He also wears a practical shirt with two breast pockets and a black leather jacket that he took with him before they left earth.

Joanna appears from their chamber; she has changed her clothes to something that looks like it's taken directly from a Hollywood movie in which the story is around a famous and tough adventurer about to go on a dangerous mission to unlock the secrets hidden in a previously unknown tomb. Henrik nods approvingly towards her with his eyebrows raised, small wrinkles appear on his forehead and the outer part of his lips points downwards as he sees her walking alluringly slowly towards him. His chest moves outwards, belly inwards and his back straightens as he tries to look as tough as he can be, but the only thing he can say sounds as cliché as cliché can get as soon as he opens his mouth. Her beauty does that to him every time and she is aware of it.

"My love, to see you is like seeing the sun for the first time; you light the fire in my heart."

Joanna who has always appreciated his quirky pickup lines, gives him a wink with her right eye as an equally quirky response as she at the same time said.

"Thank you, sweetheart, you don't look so bad either. And now we are ready for the mission, my love. Let's rescue your mother."

Henrik puts his arms around her waist as they both begin to walk to the shuttle, whistling a tune he sometimes repeats for himself when his mind wanders. They soon reach the area. Bjorn, Sofie and Serge has cleared out the shuttle, stripped it down to only the very essential parts to be able to fit the pod inside it, and at the same time have enough room to move along the inside if the need to land would confront them on the mission.

"Good, now that you two are here we can begin; shall we proceed as planned Henrik?" Serge says.

"Great to see you, Serge, I see that the shuttle has been altered, why is that?" Henrik asks, Serge just smiles as an answer before Sofie jumps in.

"Glad you asked, Henrik, you will soon find out," she says with a cheerful voice.

"I see, well then." Henrik makes a short pause as he wonders what the reason can be for the lack of answer given by her.

"I trust you on this Sofie, but I must insist that you tell me the reason. It's my mother that we are about to rescue today. So, tell me now the reason so we can begin," Henrik says. His posture has developed into a more powerful presence as a captain and he can now, when he wants to, use this newly found ability to get the answers he wants from people. Sofie would prefer to see the look on

Henrik's eyes as Anvu's pod comes in through the shuttle's rear hatch, but she gives in and reluctantly begins to answer his question.

"Ok, Henrik, I hear you. I'll tell you the reason, but I will keep only the final little trick up my sleeve to myself if that's ok?"

Henrik nods and says, "Sure thing, please tell me now."

"We stripped away the shuttle of everything to fit her pod inside. We will fly away with your mother," Sofie says as she holds the shuttle door open for them to board. Henrik's eyebrows raise as he imagines the pod swooshing in through the rear hatch.

"Didn't expect that the pod would fit inside, but this intrigues me, Sofie," Henrik says as he enters the pod. Sofie simply smiles towards him as she moves towards the cockpit.

"It will be very interesting to see how much space will be left in here when the pod enters. Hope you two can suck your bellies in," Serge says in his usual gentle way as he tries to be funny in a manner that doesn't really suit him well. Henrik and Bjorn can't take him seriously, as he is the largest person in the crew. They both begin to ironically stand in a military stance next to each other, belly in, chest out as they hold their laughter in.

Serge takes a deep breath and shakes his head

as he slowly exhales. Bjorn and Henrik relax their stance and seat themselves down on the shuttle's seats.

"Just forget what I said. Let's focus on the mission," Serge says, slightly annoyed.

"I must admit that my belly has seen better days, Serge. It doesn't show now, but there used to be some kind of developed abs there once upon a time," Bjorn says a bit ironically.

Sofie seats herself on the pilot's seat and starts the warm-up sequence with the flick of a red button on the dashboard. Joanna is seated next to her in the co-pilot's seat, casually inspecting the layout of the dashboard. She has found herself more and more interested in the mechanics around her. She is curious about how this particular shuttle works, as almost every shuttle has some sort of makeshift solutions. They are all composed of a concoction of different parts that combined, provide the functionality desired for the purpose. Sofie notices the newly found curiosity Joanna has and begins to describe what's special about this shuttle.

"I see that you find this shuttle a bit special right? Let me tell you, this particular shuttle's primary source of power comes from a relatively small dark-energy engine that produces absolutely zero noise, even when moving very large amounts of material. This is because the vibration levels of the particles that pass between the intake to the engine itself and out again have been adjusted to oscillate in a precise pattern that eliminates the surrounding sounds when the energy particles rotate asynchronously as they leave the exhaust. This provides a good enough cruising speed." When she is finished Joanna turns her head a bit to the side as she ponders something.

Sofie interrupts her thoughts to say, "I know, before you ask, I will explain. The drawback is that it can't operate unless it has gone through a rather extensive warm-up phase that might not be so practical when you want to lift off immediately. Lucky for us, we aren't in any rush at the moment." A buzzing sound, varying in pitch and loudness, is heard from the engine. "Besides, the secondary thrusters can provide additional acceleration and speed, if necessary, but only for a limited time because they don't have much fuel," Sofie adds.

"Thank you for the explanation, Sofie. When are we ready for lift-off?" Joanna asks.

"When the noise fades away, we can be sure that the engine is ready. Would you like me to guide you through it someday?"

"I would like that very much, Sofie. Maybe when we arrive back to base," Joanna replies.

"It would be my pleasure," Sofie says as she glances on the shuttle's dashboard. She sees that

Henrik and the others have positioned themselves on the foldable seats along the wall of the shuttle. She also notes that the engine warm-up has reached phase II, meaning that the particles generating the propulsion have reached the correct rotational velocity and molecular spin and can now be adjusted and finetuned accordingly to the desired vibrational pattern. She drags a few sliders on the side of the dashboard. Suddenly the noise from the engine fades away and disappears.

"Hold on in the back, it's time for lift-off," she announces just as she releases the energy clutch.

Part 26, A Mother's Embrace

The shuttle takes off, Sofie steers the vessel rapidly towards the meetup point. She is an excellent pilot who with the years have become one with the shuttles she manages. She keeps the last little trick in her sleeve hidden from the rest, only Serge knows that the shuttle's cloaking device is activated. They cruise over the rooftops of Kionidoo, soon they will arrive, a short blip on the dashboard indicates to Sofie that the target has been acquired, that the mission is on.

"I've been informed that Anvu has seated herself in the pod now and is on her way to the destination, cross your fingers that we will succeed on our mission, give me a couple of minutes and we will arrive at point Echo, pickup station," she said through the com.

"Great news. Keep us updated." Henrik looks out of the window of the shuttle as he answers her, he sees the fast display of rooftops underneath them. *This city sure looks better from a sky view rather than down on the streets, with all the despair*, Henrik reflects as he remembers the ferocious and intimidating Youllian guards he saw from the pod ride with Bjorn travelling towards the meeting place earlier.

After a while, Sofie steers the shuttle down towards the ground, smoothly landing the vehicle down on the grey asphalt at the pickup point, with the rear hatch facing the corner of the building next to them. The sun is high in the sky, and from the pilot seat, she can see the hustle outside, people and vehicles moving in a never-ending stream. On the other side of the street, near what at first glance looks like some sort of bakery, she sees that a dark grey Youllian guard pod is parked. It is marked with the military guard's symbol. She is certain that at least one guard is in there as the pod's front lights are on and it is uncommon for a guard pod to be unmanned, especially a military one. *Hopefully they won't see the disappearing pod when we take Anvu onboard*, Sofia thinks.

On the display she has followed Anvu's pod, which has passed the first checkpoint.

"Alright, so far so good, everything goes according to plan. Anvu's pod is getting near now, and I will lower the rear hatch five seconds before she arrives. Hopefully, no one will see us. Be prepared to hug the walls if you don't want to feel the sensation of being hit in the hip by a high-speed pod," she announces cheerfully as she once again points her gaze towards the guard pod across the street. *Don't do anything foolish now*, she thinks for a second, feeling the unnerving feeling of anxiety come to life. Joanna notices that she is worried about something on the outside. She peeks out and sees the pod on the other side. Not sure what kind of pod it is she assumes that it's the bad guys.

"Whatever they might be doing down there, don't overthink it, they will not be allowed to harm us in any way." Joanna's words make Sofie's hands steady again. She glances at the display once more to see that the pod is almost here now. As the pod takes its final right turn for this journey, Sofie lowers the hatch. Henrik and the others quickly hug the wall as close as they can, anticipating the swift entry of the pod through the rear. In what can only be described as an instant, the pod stops a hands-width from the cockpit's divider wall. Sofie's reaction is equally swift; she quickly takes off and redirects the pod's identification key to the prepared pod directly in front of the shuttle, her final trick up her sleeve. The pod containing Anvu's tail of two Chronos agents appears just as the newly appointed pod gains velocity and drives away towards the city centre. Sofie checks the guard pod below to see if they have been seen.

Relieved, Sofie says, "Luckily it appears that we have avoided detection, for now. I was a little bit concerned that a guard pod across the street would notice but they appear to be dormant for now, maybe the guards weren't as aware of their surroundings as they are paid to be." Sofie accelerates the shuttle forwards and begins the journey back to base. You can open the pod's hatch now. I believe we have some room left to the roof," Sofie says through the com radio.

Henrik opens the hatch, anticipating seeing his mother for the first time since his childhood. A very kind-looking woman, maybe just a little bit older than his memories, she has loving eyes that meet his as the hatch slides off the pod entirely.

Henrik finds himself speechless, all he can say is, "Hi mom, I wanted to..." his words are abruptly interrupted as Sofie takes a sharp turn, just barely avoiding a projectile that explodes in the air right behind them. Pulse beams are seen flashing by the shuttles side windows. Henrik embraces his mother so to protect her from any harm as Sofie accelerates and takes another sharp turn to avoid a second projectile from the attacker.

"They have discovered us!" Sofie yells from the cockpit. "Quickly! Grab onto something my friends; it will be a bumpy ride. I have to unplug the dampers to be able to evade fire from behind. They have somehow seen us even with the cloaking device active," she adds as the whole shuttle begins to move back and forth to make it harder for the attacker to hit them.

"Shake them off. Do what you have to do Sofie, lose them and take us back to base, hurry!" Henrik shouts as he firmly holds on to the side of the pod, the adrenaline rush of being pursued flows through his body at an increasing speed. All Henrik can think of is Joanna and his mother, the two most loved ones in his life; they must be protected at all costs. Joanna sees on the display that there is more incoming from further back.

"Faster, we have to go faster! Engage the thrusters, Sofie!" Joanna says as she tightens the belt around her waist and up to her shoulders. Sofie releases the safety switch beneath the dashboard to wake up the thrusters.

"Now you better hold on to something back there!" she yells. She counts to two to give them time to react before she pushes the button to engage the thrusters. What before felt like a bumpy ride is now a full-on fight for survival to hold on. The acceleration is felt all the way down in the chest. Sofie closely watches how the distance to the attacker increases on the display. *Come on now, give me the speed we need.* Little by little the distance between them increases and the attacker no longer fires projectiles towards them. Henrik can still see the occasional pulse beam flashing outside the shuttle, he can feel the heavy heartbeat in his chest now. Sofie's voice is heard from the cockpit.

"Come on now!"

Part 27, Lay low!

W hat feels like an eternity, only takes around ten minutes. The shuttle's thrusters are no longer engaged, and the attacker is nowhere to be seen. Sofie takes a relieved sigh as she goes in for the landing outside the base. Henrik has broadcasted through a safe channel to both bases to pack up the essential equipment in case they have to make a swift escape to *Eclipse*. The shuttle lands on the backside of the base with the rear hatch facing the entrance. Sofie opens the rear hatch and reverses the pod out from the shuttle and into the camp. They all leave the shuttle and move inside.

Through a private channel, Sofie almost whispers as she says to Henrik, "It wasn't meant that they would notice us. I just hope that they don't know who we are and especially who you are!" her voice almost disappears as they mention the possibility that they know about them. Henrik answers as calmly as he can, trying to hide his own worries.

"It's not your fault, Sofie. They obviously noticed us long before we landed on that spot. I just hope that we haven't miscalculated their ability to track us and that they have been hiding their knowledge since we first arrived." Henrik turns his head towards her as he continues, making sure to keep eye contact.

"My biggest fear is that we have another mole in our team. I just can't let that happen! Report any and all suspicious behaviour you see, my friend." His words echo in her ears with the possibility of someone else besides Loukh being an infiltrator. She opens her mouth to answer but closes it again, she instead just nods as an answer to Henrik.

"Thank you, my friend I trust, you."

Henrik turns his head towards Anvu and Joanna, who now stands beside him, he gives them both a reassuring look and in his mother's eyes he sees a calmness that is undeniably a result of a long and eventful life.

"I'm so glad that we finally meet mother. I have so many questions to ask you and so little time at the moment, but I promise you that when this situation calms down, we will sit and talk. I almost can't believe that you are here with me now at this moment," he says.

Anvu smiles back, takes her son's hand, and said, "My dear son, if you only knew how much

I have missed you throughout the years that have passed. In the beginning, after your father passed away, I was devastated and just hoped that the crew we assigned to take you far, far away from here succeeded in their mission and that you would be safe." Henrik opens his mouth to answer but Anvu stops him.

"It made me so happy when I heard through my agents that you were on the way to Zuood. I have longed for this moment since the day you were taken away. From time to time I have received news of your health and life and when I now see you here, with your stunning and courageous wife who I have also heard a lot about, and a crew that is dedicated to return this galaxy to its former glory, I can only feel a great proudness in my heart." She reaches out for Joanna's hand as well.

"You remind me of myself when I was young, my dear Joanna, I know it's the first time we meet, but I have seen you so many times in the intel I've received from Bjorn that it feels like I have known you for a long time," Anvu says.

Joanna smiles and answers her newly found mother-in-law. "Thank you for your kind words. I'm so happy to finally meet you too, Anvu. Let's move further inside the base. I bet that you are at least as hungry as I am."

On their way to the lunch area, they pass a few

boxes that are left on the ground in a hurry as the crew filled the shuttles earlier.

Viterin is heard through the com radio. "I'm not sure what kind of mess you have made over there, but we are ready to leave on your orders."

"Good. Stay put for now, my friend. We are still unsure what our next move will be. We need to stay low for a while and secure our plan," Henrik replies.

They sit down on the makeshift benches to enjoy their meal. It can only be described as a bowl filled with something similar to thick noodles and meat in a broth that has just a pinch of saffron added to it.

Part 28, Gather intelligence!

A s the last piece of meat stew leaves the bowl, Anvu takes out some sort of small blue piece of gadget. It has the size and feel of a USB stick, but it lacks any visible plug.

"If someone ever thought that I was just relaxing during these long years like a sad old lady, then they could be more wrong," she says as she puts the gadget on the table. Henrik and Joanna looks curiously at the device.

"I don't think anyone ever thought that about you, Anvu," Joanna replies. Anvu points towards the device with her palm facing the ceiling.

"Maybe so, dear, but let me explain what I have been occupied with all these years," Anvu takes a short pause, letting their curiosity around the device ripen.

"I have devoted myself to finding out every little bit of information about Tidus Barlow and his Chronos Corporation. I collected intel and made plans in the dark for how to best take them out.

Most of that information is contained in this data crystal."

"I see, Anvu, you have been very diligent, just as I always believed you were from what I have heard and from what I can remember from my childhood when I often played with Henrik in your home." When Bjorn is finished, Anvu gives him a thankful smile for a second before she returns her attention towards the matter at hand.

"Thank you, Bjorn for your kind words. Yes, as I told you before, I haven't been lazy. Just before you arrived, I received some very interesting information that I believe will complete the data so we can begin to build a strong plan that will surely put an end to the era of Tidus. Take this crystal and keep it safe, we will need it soon." Anvu reaches for the crystal, giving it to Henrik.

"I will keep it safe, Mother, I promise," he says. He takes the crystal and gently puts it in his left shirt pocket.

"What was the information you were given? And what do we need to do?" he curiously asks.

"Of course, my dear son, the last piece of information we need is stored in a similar device as the one you just received. It is located in one of Chronos buildings on the northern outskirts of Kionidoo. We must do all that we can to get our hands on this device. You see, this I believe will show very specific information of Tidus' whereabouts, his inner circle, and his resources." Anvu emphasizes the name with a dark tone.

"Tidus"

"What do you mean? Is the coward in hiding? Why don't we know his whereabouts?" Bjorn asks.

"You are correct as always, my dear Bjorn. Tidus himself hasn't been seen in public, or for that matter anywhere else. for a very long time. We believe that he stills lives somewhere here on the planet, but we simply aren't sure," Anvu says. Henrik is inspired by his mother's natural ability to talk and move people as a leader. He is proud, and it can be seen on him as he looks her lovingly in the eyes.

He begins to ask a question that lingers on his tongue. "As you say, mother. We must find him and make him account for all his tyranny, where exactly is this device located? And how will we snatch it from them?" In Henrik's mind, a plan begins to emerge, but he can't be sure until he knows all that he needs to know.

"That's the hard part, I guess. All my agents have with time been compromised, they can't move freely around anymore so our hope lies on a small team that silently enters the building, grabs the device and swiftly returns with it, then we need to leave this planet for a while." Anvu answers.

"Leave this planet?" Bjorn asks.

"We can't stay on this planet any longer. The Alliance have a secret base in another star system that we will use to build our strength and our numbers. It's located in the Taolak system a few lightyears away from here, so we need to prepare your ship for an immediate jump when we arrive. Yo-Kiel who I heard that you meet before, is in charge of the base," Anvu says.

"I understand. I will make sure that all the necessary preparations are made right away." Bjorn takes out a device from his pocket and begins to send encrypted instructions to *Eclipse*. As he does so, Joanna leaps up from the bench. In her eyes, Henrik sees a fire that he knows all too well. This energy is the last piece needed for the plan in Henrik's head to work, she begins to say.

"I volunteer for the mission. Me and one more can easily take a shuttle and infiltrate the building. It will be hard, but I am quick on my feet and will be able to retrieve the device." Joanna turns to Sofie. "I need the best pilot I know by my side. Will you accompany me on the mission, Sofie?" She knows that Sofie isn't hard to convince when it comes to going out on missions.

"Of course, I will my friend! To fly is my passion and I wouldn't want you to fly with someone else on this important mission. Let's do it." She is on her feet now next to Joanna. Henrik looks pleased with the outcome, as does Bjorn as he faces Henrik's eyes. In his mind, the plan was already set like this. He leans back on the bench and puts his palms forward and upwards.

"I'm glad that you two volunteered. You're perfect for this mission, I agree, so let's hear the details of the plan. When, where, and how?" Bjorn asks.

Anvu places a round disk on the table. Out from it, a blue light begins to display a hologram of a building. She goes through the plan that she and her agents have worked on, every detail is discussed and revisited until perfection.

"It's a simple and hands-on plan on the surface actually," she begins. "The device is believed to be located deep inside a research facility where Chronos used to experiment with the time dilation device they received from the Youllian." The hologram splits the building in the middle, showing a pathway into the inner rooms of the facility.

"It shouldn't be heavily guarded, but there's always a couple of guards keeping a check on the facility. According to the intelligence we've received, there could still be some sort of research activity being conducted," Anvu says.

"What kind of activity are we talking about, Mother?" Henrik asks.

"To be honest we are unsure. The tiny amount of information we've been able to collect doesn't reveal too much. All we know at the moment is that several boxes are delivered each week and some personnel wear a kind of protective equipment." She turns off the disk and hands it over to Joanna as Henrik nods in agreement.

"Well then what are we waiting for?"

"Joanna and Sofie, I need you to prepare the shuttle for this new stealth mission. Be extra careful and study the holodisk for the best landing position. I know I can count on your bright heads to figure out the best approach." Joanna is still standing next to the bench, leaning slightly forward as her hands are supporting her against the table. Her eyes are fixed on the disk as she goes through a plan that has begun to take shape in her mind. Henrik's question doesn't take away her concentration; in fact, it enhances it as she answers him.

"Of course, my dear. We will begin the preparations right away. In my mind, we are already at the facility with the device in our hands."

Part 29, The research facility!

S ofie steers the shuttle over the clouds. In front of her, she sees the stunningly beautiful sunrise that paints the horizon in a warm and almost touchable pink shade. They are on their way towards the facility and she feels exhausted. They were up all night preparing the shuttle and developing their plan. Joanna found a very good spot for them to land, which is adjacent to a corridor near a loading dock that hopefully will be slightly less guarded so they can sneak in unseen.

Meanwhile, Henrik and the rest of the crew have packed up what they can during the night and positioned it inside the secondary shuttle. A few boxes are left on the floor and nothing has been done to hide the eventual leftovers of the base. As Henrik walks towards the crew who are eating breakfast, he can feel the tension in the room as the crew sits in silence while they slowly chew on their food.

"hrm hrm." Henrik clears his throat to get their

attention. "My dear companions, my brave champions, my strong crew of the greatest starship that I at least ever been inside." He waits for them to focus a bit more and sit straighter on the benches, as their posture gets better, he continues.

"Don't feel the fatigue just yet, as we still have a rough time ahead of us. We will return to *Eclipse* in a few hours and I need you to recharge your energy for now. My dear wife Joanna and Bjorn's resourceful daughter Sofie left this base a few minutes ago to secure the last piece we need to overthrow Tidus and his corrupt Chronos Corporation." He sees a few nods and even a pair of raised fists in the air, they are beginning to feel their moral recover, with renewed strength and higher tone he continues.

"We will build our strength and number in the Taolak system and, when we are ready, we will return and strike both harsh and swiftly at the very heart of Tidus and remove his reign from this incredible planet, from this entire galaxy! This is our Andromeda, our Zuood!"

They cheer and shout with all their fists in the air, Henrik is pleased with their morale.

Over the clouds on the far north side of Kionidoo, Sofie begins to manoeuvre the shuttle down towards the ground. They are almost in position.

"Joanna, we are closing in at the landing site now.

Keep a lookout for any eventual guards near the area," she says as they descend. They can now see the building in front of them, but it's still too far away for them to distinguish any details on the ground.

"I'll keep my eye out for anything suspicious looking. On our way here, I've been searching on the ledger we recovered from the Man O'Warship, in hope to find something of interest regarding this building. Perhaps someone made a signature or left some sort of information we could use. I'm not surprised that there's a lack of information though," Joanna answers. She puts down the shuttle's tablet-sized datapad and readjusts the seat to better be able to search the perimeter of the facility.

"Great idea, my friend. The recovered ledger hasn't unfolded that many secrets from the future so far, but we should definitely keep using it. As you say, it might be something hidden inside the blocks," Sofie says. She turns the shuttle gently to the right to begin the final descent to the infiltration spot. They now have the research facility straight in front of them. The facility building dominates the entire view. On the roof they see huge metallic pipes going over each other, crossing from one side to the other and down again. A black spire on top of a pyramid-shaped structure sticks out on the far-left side and an impressive battery of pulse cannons are positioned in every corner of the facility.

"This facility is well-armed, to say the least. There must be something incredibly important inside indeed," Joanna points out. As she explores the building top to bottom, she counts at least seven floors and notices that the plain grey, almost boring facade of the building doesn't give away so much of its intended function. Her eyes leave the facade and she looks further down onto the building's yard, a fortified gate with adjacent watchtowers all along the perimeter surrounds it. No lights are seen inside any of the towers.

Joanna's sharp eyes carefully scan the ground, the windows, and the roof for anything noticeable; all is quiet. She quickly locates the spot where they are to land on the right side of the building a few steps away from a loading dock for goods. As the shuttle gently touches the ground, Joanna moves from the co-pilot seat and back to the side door. She picks up a backpack with equipment that they previously stuffed inside the shuttle. Joanna removes two items and gives one of them to Sofie.

"Here, take this and holster it. I am sure we will need them; don't worry, they are set to stun," she says as Sofie grabs the pulse-gun with her right hand. She leaves the seat and, with the gun in her hand, she smilingly answers.

"You have grown into your role well, my friend. I bet that you one day will prove to be a leader of your own in some form, your way of speaking has drastically shifted to a more authoritative tone when serious business awaits." Sofie holsters her gun on the right side of her hip.

"Maybe so my dear, maybe so." Joanna slowly opens the side door and puts the bag on her back, hanging from one of her shoulders. As she walks out, she marks the spot just below the door with her boot, leaving a slightly visible line on the ground so they can find the cloaked shuttle quickly if needed. Outside, everything is silent except the slightly muffled noises of the city itself and the sound of steel being hammered from a nearby construction site a few blocks away. Sofie closes the door as she leaves it, making their entry complete. The air is cool against their cheeks as they approach the loading dock's first door. With one hand on the holster and a crowbar in the other, Joanna is ready to break into the facility. Sofie has a nipper to disengage the alarm. They move fast across the yard, constantly scanning the surrounding back and forth. It doesn't take long until they reach the door. After inspecting the door for a moment, Sofie concludes that they can proceed.

"The door is thick, but from the looks of it we

are in a bit of luck. The alarm that they have used on this facility isn't the most reliable. Hand me the bag, Joanna." Sofie picks out a small, black device and puts it beside the handle, explaining that a narrow line of lights on the device indicates the strength of the magnetic alarm and where it is located on the door frame. Sofie picks up another smaller device and positions it a bit above the handle next to the frame.

"Okay, let's try if this will work, as soon as you force the door open with the crowbar, I will slide this device in between the door and the doorframe. It will be visible that the door is tampered with, so we must hurry in case someone sees the door," Sofie whispers. Joanna is more than ready with the crowbar, and with a forceful stab she hits the minuscule gap that the frame allows. The crowbar gets a grip and with all her strength she bends the door slightly open. A crack is heard, and the door gives way.

"Impressive, my friend," Sofie whispers. They both enter the facility, placing the items back into the backpack, unholstering the guns, and turning on the mounted flashlights, as the corridor isn't lit.

"We know what we have to do now. The device should be located a few floors down, so let's find the stairwell and stay alert for anything that moves. Better to stun than to be caught in the act," Joanna whispers and points with her hand in the direction they should move.

Part 30, The cost of success!

T he corridor that they stand in looks abandoned. When they move further in, they see
open doors that are leading into empty rooms on
either side of the corridor. As they walk, leave
footprints around the dusty floor behind them.

"At least we can be quite sure that this corridor
hasn't seen any action in a long time, nobody even
walks on this floor anymore," Joanna says. Her
flashlight keeps moving from side to side in the
corridor, but now, as the sunlight slowly begins to
brighten their way as it floods in from the windows,
they turn off the flashlights and continue in silence
further in, keeping a firm grip on the gun's handle.
On the doors they pass, they see number plates
that ascend the further in they go, and Joanna
remembers what Anvu told them about the facility,
that they tested the time dilation device in this
building.

"Wonder if this floor was some kind of ward for
their test subjects during the development phase

of the device?" she whispers, carelessly thinking aloud to herself rather than as a direct question to Sofie.

"I bet you are right my friend. This corridor really sends me shivers down my spine. I don't want to think about the gruesome things that might have happened in these rooms," Sofie remarks as they reach a closed double door.

"This might be the stairwell, let's check it out." Joanna grabs the door handle and pulls the door open. On the other side, they swiftly make their way downstairs, taking quick steps on the stairwell that horrifyingly consist of a metal mesh that allows one to see all the way down to the bottom of the stairwell. They pass by doors marked with weird, old Zuoodi symbols on their way down.

After the third door Joanna stops. "How are we supposed to figure out which floor we should explore further? Can you read the symbols?" she asks. The door in front of them contains two symbols; one that looks like a vortex of sorts and one square with three of the edges cut, and three for Joanna recognizable symbols are seen as well underneath the first symbols.

"No, unfortunately, I can't read the upper symbols, my friend. They are too old for me to interpret, but from the word written in newer Zuoodi, I can read the word Olak, which doesn't make much sense as it means bread. So I guess we just have to try one door and see what's on the other side," Sofie says.

They slowly push the door open, making sure to produce as little noise as possible. The corridor they enter appears to be empty; no sounds are heard. The walls on this floor are hospital white, and along the floor, a ribbed track runs in the middle. Joanna wonders for a second what those tracks are for. Further in, they see square boxes covered with an oversized grey fabric cover that spreads a bit out over the floor. Past the boxes and in through an open door, they see a few beds similar to those you see in hospitals pressed against each other in a narrow room.

"What exactly happened here? The further in we go, the worse it gets. Chronos has done some nasty stuff, that I'm sure of, but I have never thought that it would be this dark," Sofie says with a tired voice. Something moves in front of them, a shadow on the wall further ahead. Joanna clenches her fist in the air to signal silence and to take a crouching position. The shadow in front of them becomes smaller and eventually disappears towards the floor. She gives a signal to slowly move forward.

Does the shadow belong to a guard or a scientist? More than one? Joanna thinks as their steps take them closer to the origin of the shadow. They see now that the shadow is cast from a lit room just a few steps in front of them. When they reach the door frame, they discreetly peek inside, seeing three people dressed in grey coats handling something on a table in the middle of the room. At the far left in the corner a tall and athletically muscular Youllian guard carelessly brushes away dirt from his boots and onto the already dirty floor, beside him a dim light can be seen from a display. The grey coats move away from the table, open a door on the other side and walks into an adjacent room, discussing something inaudible. The guard is quick to follow and as the door shuts the room is silent.

"Quickly now, we must take this opportunity and see what is shown on the display," Joanna whispers. With light steps they make their way towards the light, Sofie holsters her gun and begins to interact with the display.

"Keep an eye and ear out if anyone approaches. I'll try to see if we can get a more accurate idea of how this facility is organized," she whispers. Joanna holds a steady aim at the door. A few minutes go by. The door is still and they both hold their mouth shut so that they can avoid any unnecessary noise that might attract attention.

"Finally," Sofie softly says. Joanna holds her gaze towards the door as she answers.

"What have you found, my friend?"

"The key to our mission. Let's move out quietly. I believe that the area we need to investigate is one floor further down. I noted the private key that gives us access to open the door downstairs and added it into my chip for easy access."

"That's genius! Let's move," Joanna says. When they leave the room, they quickly return to the stairwell. The door one floor down contains a triangle with a circle above. Next to the symbol, the word Liak is imprinted in Zuoodi.

"Okay, this makes at least a bit more sense to me. The word Liak means library," Sofie says with increased certainty that they are on the right path. The door is locked, but as Sofie waves her right hand in front of a reader on the wall, the door unlocks. With ease, she pushes the door open. Inside they see row after row of empty shelves. Only on one shelf Sofie notices a blue book with silver text, leaning against the side of the shelf in its loneliness, the rest are empty and dust filled.

"They could certainly begin to stock up on books in this library," Sofie chuckles; she can't help it. Joanna holds her laughter and points towards a glimmer of light at the end of one of the rows.

"What's that? We should move over there," she says, not entirely sure on the importance of the glimmer but with a gut feeling that she at this moment can't be wrong. With a steady grip on their weapons, they push forward. The light comes from a room filled with displays of all sorts, old static next to the latest models of holoscreens. A desk is next to the displays and what looks like a server is incorporated into the wall on the right side of the desk. Sofie positions herself in front of the screens. She cracks her neck just enough to produce a pleasing relief, a satisfactory warm feeling all along her upper spine gives her the relaxation she needs as she begins to search for anything interesting in the database. Joanna watches in fascination while text in old Zuoodi rolls past on the screens, Sofie is really in her element right now in front of the screens and it does not take long before she manages to identify where the device is located.

"I think I have found it, we are in the correct room and it should be plugged into this particular access point, let me see...ah yes it opens." Sofie pulls a sliding door next to the server rack and checks to see if any external devices are plugged in. From Joanna's limited knowledge of how server rooms look Earth, this rack reminds her of exactly that. Behind the rack, several cables are connected in the same disorganized, confusing way as she has seen on pictures. Sofie mutters something muffled to herself as she bends further back behind the hardware.

"Have you found the device, Sofie?" Joanna asks. Sofie once again mutters something, Joanna can't hear what she said, so she returns her attention towards the surroundings instead. Sofie is almost crawling on the floor behind the racks as she finally identifies the correct device and reaches for it with her right hand. When she removes the device from the access point, an alarm begins to sound.

"Crap! We have to run! Here, take the device and hold on to it tight. Now move, move, move," Sofie yells as she knows that the time to be subtle and cautious is over, they begin to run towards the stairwell once more. "Quickly! We have to reach the shuttle as fast as we can. We don't know how many guards are in this building, but I am sure they are all on their way towards us right now," Sofie says as she runs behind Joanna who reaches the door first and kicks it open with her right foot.

They have holstered their weapons to run faster. Without looking back, they take double steps up the stairs. As they reach the floor they first landed on, they hear doors below them getting kicked in and guards yelling at each other in some unknown language. They run into the half-lit corridor. Suddenly, guards appear from a corner in front of them. Joanna grabs Sofie's arm and jumps into an empty room for shelter. The guard notices and shots are fired towards them. The whole corridor explodes with light as the green projectiles travel the short distance from the corner to the doorframe. A burst of shots hits the door frame and several even manage to go into the room at an angle.

"Be ready. As soon as they pause, we jump out and take our shots. Aim well," Joanna says. She tries to keep her pulse steady, as she can feel her heartbeat heavy against her chest. Finally the guards stop shooting for a second. Joanna takes her chance and jumps out. Time seems to almost stand still as she takes the shots, three rapid bursts aimed directly at the guards.

"Come, they are all down let's run for it," Joanna shouts, and they run as fast as they can towards the door they came from. Sofie reaches it first and knocks it open with her right shoulder. The sunlight hits them both in the eyes. Its bright shine has transformed the dull loading dock into a display of colours.

"What's that? Shield?" Joanna shouts as she sees a glimmering wave in the air above the facility's outer court wall, which glows villainously at them.

"I guess so," Sofie says as she runs towards the marking on the ground where the shuttle should be. She activates the side door to open. Joanna turns around just before she reaches the shuttle as Sofie takes a last leap and enters the shuttle and hurries to get inside the pilot seat. Joanna's face freezes as a projectile barely misses her face. A guard is running towards them, she draws her pulse gun once more from the holster and takes a final shot, making the guard squeal in pain as she hits him in his right shoulder; he twists before hitting the ground. A fitting end for his career, she thinks as she jumps inside the shuttle just before Sofie accelerates sharply and the shuttle lifts off

Sofie knows that they won't be able to get away quickly enough to avoid all the incoming fire, but at least the shuttle should be able to penetrate the shield, or so she believes. Sofie clenches her fist and steers in a half-eight pattern, hoping for the best. The Youllian forces fire from several angles. The cannon battery on the roof isn't late for the party, as several projectiles flash by the shuttle.

"Hold on to anything you can. I will try to get us out of here alive," Sofie shouts as she accelerates to maximum velocity, the whole shuttle shakes as the thrusters fire. Joanna is pushed against the rear hatch; the force of the acceleration is almost unbearable.

"Hold tight!" Sofie yells as she sees a Youllian fighter vessel come towards them from the front. Her view is filled with the sinister light of a projectile coming straight at them.

"We have incomi..." a terrible noise fills Joanna's

entire world as a projectile rips apart the front of the shuttle. The deafening sound of turbulence combined with the sensation of falling takes her out of consciousness and the shuttle crashes down to the streets below.

Part 31, Rescue mission!

H enrik who has followed the shuttle since he got the message that Joanna and Sofie had to escape from the building, is beside himself with worry. His heart feels like it has been torn out with a red-hot knife when he sees on the secondary shuttle's screen how the shuttle's status changes to "lost." He feels faint and his mournful cries echoes throughout the camp. Bjorn falls to his knees, unable to breathe. Anvu slams her fist on the wall as hard as she can, the sound disrupts their thoughts, they quickly re-enter reality once more. Henrik tries to reach them through the com radio.

"Joanna...My love! Please respond if you are alive!" the signal from her gear is faint but at least they still have a signal. Bjorn contacts Viterin through a secure connection.

"Viterin! Send your shuttle to the crash site immediately."

Viterin is quick to respond. "Already on my way. We will take them both back with us, even if it will be the last thing we do." Viterin's confident voice soothes them a little bit.

As Viterin's shuttle makes its way towards the crash site, Henrik orders his shuttle to lift off. Serge is quick to respond and jumps into the pilot seat.

"Fasten yourself and hold on; this will be a rough ride," he says as he pushes the throttle forward, engaging the shuttle's engine to lift off. No response is heard from Joanna or Sofie as Henrik and Viterin's shuttle quickly approaches the site. Viterin is a couple of minutes from the site. As he gets closer, he sees black smoke rising from a residential neighbourhood.

"I'm at the site now, going down to the ground," he reports through the line. The commotion of the crash has garnered a reasonable amount of attention and the ground is filled with people watching in fascination. Viterin sees a few guards on the ground as well. He turns his head backwards to tell the other guys in the shuttle to prepare for fire.

"On my mark, we go down and open fire on anything that can even remotely be a threat to us. Two of you jump out and grab the girls, alive or dead." The last words leave a salty taste on his tongue. He opens both the side doors and the rear hatch; with a swift manoeuvre, he now hovers above the wreckage. The crew onboard lights the sky with fire against the Youllian guard patrols, who all go down. Viterin makes his move to the ground with a 180-degree turn that positions the rear hatch just in front of the crashed shuttle.

Nyana and Hyat, two of Viterin's most veteran crewmembers, jump out through the rear hatch. The scene they enter is unlike anything they have ever seen before. The shuttle's driver seat is completely blown away. Neither Sofie nor her body can be found. They jump inside the shuttle to see that Joanna lies unconscious at the very end, with her backpack in a tight grip around her waist.

"We have sights on Joanna. She looks to be alive, unfortunately, we have no signs of Sofie, she isn't in here or around the crash site," Hyat reports to Viterin as he turns around to give Nyana cover while she gently lifts Joanna in her arms, carries her past the burnt interior, and make sure to avoid all the debris on the floor on the way out. Her last steps lead her past where Sofie should have been and her thoughts go to Bjorn who will probably never see his daughter again.

"We have secured Joanna; she is unconscious but alive and in need of immediate medical attention," Viterin reports through the secured com radio as he lifts off from the ground. Henrik draws a sigh of relief as he hears that Joanna is alive and at the same time his heart fills once again with anxiety over her health *Stay strong my love, I will soon be by your side.*

Viterin hesitates for a second, unsure of how to tell Bjorn that his only daughter wasn't found at the crash site; the silence makes Bjorn cry out.

"What about Sofie?!" Bjorn cries, unable to stand, his voice shaky and filled with anxiety. Henrik grabs a reassuring hold of Bjorn's shoulders. Viterin takes a deep breath and exhales; he knows that his next words will give his closest friend grief so immeasurably great that he most likely will never fully recover. Of course, there's still a minuscule chance that Sofie miraculously survived somehow, but it's a chance so small that it doesn't even make sense. Viterin shakes his head a couple of times to calm his nerves

"Bjorn, it's with my deepest regret and utmost respect that I, unfortunately, have to give you the news, be assured that we did all that we can and all that.." Bjorn crashes, the rest of the words Viterin said blur into oblivion, his head feels like it will explode and at the same time it is completely hollow. Henrik holds his dear friend steady in his arms as tears begin to flow for everyone aboard both shuttles. Bjorn shakes uncontrollably while he sits hunched over on the floor with one hand pressed against his forehead, the other lies limp on the floor.

Henrik manages to tear himself out of grief and

gathers himself enough to give the order to flee towards *Eclipse*. Serge, who has kept the shuttle at a safe distance slowly circling around a couple of rooftops, makes sure everyone is seated. Henrik helps Bjorn into his seat and fastens him down; his eyes are empty and barren. As soon as Serge is sure they are all secured, he presses the throttle once more to maximum, sets the course towards *Eclipse*. Seconds later he engages the external thrusters.

The acceleration presses everyone against their seats as it reaches transonic speed. The shuttle vibrates like it will burst into flames any second and the sound of metal plates vibrating overwhelms one's thoughts. Henrik makes eye contact with Anvu who, with tears still running down her cheeks, gives him a reassuring look that gets his nerves to calm down further. All they need to succeed in now for the moment is to get back to *Eclipse* in one piece. A few moments later, the sound and vibration fade away as they leave the atmosphere. Henrik allow himself once more to worry about his beloved; his heart bleeds with anxiety.

Part 32, Jump to Taolak!

O nce back on *Eclipse* they must hurry. Henrik is fully aware that Tidus and his thugs might well have figured out who they are and that they are coming after them to crush the resistance before even fully started. Viterin arrived shortly before Henrik. As they landed, Joanna was taken directly to sickbay, Henrik having ordered the crew to make the jump to Taolak at once. Anvu takes care of Bjorn. With a soft and loving voice she tells Henrik that she will sit with him until he can stand on his feet once more.

"Go, my son, find Joanna and give her the strength she needs. Go now." Henrik gives his mother a quick embrace and runs as fast as he can towards the infirmary. His heart beating heavily in his chest and it feels like it will take an eternity, until he finally pushes the door open and sees his beloved wife. She is bruised up and lying unconscious on a bed. Several surround around her, finishing the plaster around her broken leg.

An IV drip stand is positioned near the bed. Henrik sits next to her and takes her hand in his. Her head is wrapped with a bandage. Nyana, who took Joanna from the shuttle and into the room, lays her hand on Henrik's shoulder to reassure him that everything will be ok.

"She is remarkably strong. I didn't think anyone could survive the crash. She will be ok Henrik, just give it some time," she says. Henrik sits in silence as he listens to the high-pitched tone generated from the machine that monitors Joanna's heartbeat. The steady rhythm at least allows him to calm down a bit. He's always aware that the situation can change at any time, but it makes him feel more confident that she will make it.

The now-familiar sensation of jumping into hyperdrive passes his body for a split second, he is relieved that they have left Zuood for now. Henrik sits beside Joanna for several hours until exhaustion catches up with him and he falls asleep with his head against the bed beside her pillow. Anvu enters the room and when she sees that they are both breathing, she takes a sigh of relief.

Anvu leans against the doorframe as she reflects on the short time since she has been reunited with her son. She has longed for this moment for so long; and now it finally has become her reality. For most of her life, she has worked for the Alliance, together with Mato until his early passing. *So much pain we all have to endure during our life to secure the Alliance rebirth*, she thinks. A tear runs from her right eye and down her cheek when she turns around to leave the room, giving them time to heal and rest.

Bjorn is sitting together with Davood and Viterin in a secluded corner of the bridge; the mood is tense and mournful. On the table in front of them, they each have a small glass of whiskey to calm the nerves, a smooth and smoky bottle of Lagavulin. Bjorn had saved it for Sofie's birthday, as he knew how much she enjoyed the smokey taste and feel of the fine whiskey. The first shock after realizing that his beloved daughter died in the crash slowly has slowly begun to settle with Bjorn. At first, he couldn't talk or respond to any attempt to get an answer out of him. Now he nods or shakes his head as Davood and Viterin gently talk to him.

"Your daughter was the bravest of them all, old friend," Viterin says, holding the whiskey in front of him, giving it a gentle swirl before he continues. "Everyone loved her, and we will give her the farewell that she deserves, she was a daughter to us all."

Davood lifts his glass as well, holding it steady in front of him, mirroring Viterin's movement. With a sad and heavy voice he says, "This is a time to reflect on life, how fragile it can be and how important it is to remember our loved ones as the amazing people they were." Davood invites Bjorn to lift his glass, so he does and now three glasses are in the air.

"She was the greatest mechanic and pilot I've ever known. There wasn't anything that she couldn't fix or any issue she couldn't solve." Davood proudly says. With grief, sadness, and Sofie's face in their mind, together they raise their glasses further.

Bjorn, with tears running down his cheeks, says, "This drink is for you, my sweet daughter. I can't believe that you are gone. You will forever be by my side; always living, you will forever be remembered as a person filled with life, a smile that could raise the mood in any room and any situation." They let the whiskey run down their lips to fill their mouth with temporary relief.

Joanna slowly but steadily opens her eyes. She wants to move but can feel her fatigue all through her body. All she can do is to slowly turn her head. The sight of Henrik breathing slowly next to her fills her heart with warmth. With a dry throat she tries to wake him up; she wonders where Sofie is.

"Henrik, wake up...I'm here." She can feel his hand around hers, so she squeezes it with the strength that she has left even though it hurts. With a confused look on his face, Henrik sees Joanna's deep and loving eyes. He smiles and keeps his hand tightly around her as he rises from the pillow into a sitting position beside her. Her cheeks are bruised and a dark spot on the bandage around her head signals that it needs to be changed, so he calls for help outside the room. Nyana, who has kept an almost constant watch over her, comes in almost without a delay. She smiles towards them and gently removes the bandages, making sure to have a clean cloth ready beside her. As the bandages are removed, Joanna keeps her eyes closed; she is tired and weary. She remembers very little about how she ended up in this bed.

Did we succeed with the mission? What about Sofie? She wonders. Henrik sees the worried expression on her face.

It's not yet time to tell her, let her rest, he thinks, unsure how he will tell her that Sofie is gone. He decides that the best action right now is to let his wife rest and inform her later. He places his right hand on her thigh and presses gently with his fingers.

"Don't worry about anything else other than your rest and healing. Everything will be ok in the end my love, I promise." Joanna relaxes a bit more in her bed as she hears his reassuring words. A fresh, cold cotton cloth is placed on her head by Nyana, feeling a stinging sensation when the liquid on the cloth touches her wounds. The feeling disappears as quickly as it arose, she opens her eyes once more to find that she is now sitting up in her bed without her noticing the bed moving. With her hands lying beside her, she can feel how the plaster around her leg begins to itch. Henrik's smile gives her the needed strength to calm her nerves, Nyana removes the cloth on her head and takes out a fresh package of bandages.

"I'll just re-wrap your head, dear, and I will be finished with you for now so you can rest."

Joanna smiles as a response. All she wants to do right now is to sleep a little more. When she is finished, Nyana adjusts the pillow behind Joanna's head, making sure that she sits comfortably as she lowers the bed once more and leaves the room as swiftly as she entered.

"Rest now, my love, I'm here by your side." Henrik kisses her and gently caresses her cheek as she falls asleep.

Part 33, Moment of remembrance and farewell!

A few days have passed. *Eclipse* arrived at the Taolak system without anyone following them and the ship has been sheltered behind an asteroid on the edge of the system. Preparations for a final farewell for Sofie have been the focus for them all, a last tribute to the friend before they continue on their journey. General Yo-Kiel contacted them as soon as they arrived at the Taolak system via a secure link to confirm the place where they shall meet. The base is hidden and located on Nauvis, a rust-red planet in the system. There, they will meet all the leaders of the Alliance and lay the foundations for the battle, gathering their forces into a strong, formidable army that can overthrow Tidus' empire.

Joanna is out of her bed now with Henrik by her side. They are in their quarters and he is fiddling with a cube. For the moment, Joanna is restricted to a wheelchair, but Nyana told her that with a newly improved procedure, the fracture will soon be completely healed. The thought of being able to walk again makes her joyful and filled with hope. The feeling is short as everything around her reminds her that Sofie didn't make it

She tilts her head towards Henrik and says, "It's not right you know."

Henrik lifts his head from what he was doing on the cube and nods in her direction. "I know, my love."

Joanna rolls the chair closer to him.

"The news that Sofie didn't make it in the crash felt so terrible when you finally revealed it to me, Henrik. I understand why, my love but the way I heard about it wasn't the right way. I thought that it couldn't be true and that Sofie would pop her head around a corner somewhere in an attempt to make some kind of wicked practical joke." Henrik's heart feels heavy as he sees her teary eyes filled with sorrow and loss.

He quietly lays the cube back on its docking station and turns all his attention towards her and says, "My love, I know you are hurt, and that the news reached you in a way that I didn't foresee. I wanted you to focus on your recovery in peace and without too much worry. It was hard to see you bruised up and plastered in bed." Joanna exhales loudly as her shoulders sags and she points her head down at the floor. Down her cheeks salty tears travel and fall in tiny drops as they reach the edge of her chin. Henrik walks over to her, crouches down beside her, and takes both her hands in a gentle grip.

"My heartbeat has never pumped so hard yet felt like it stopped completely at the same time when we saw the shuttle going down and we lost the signal. It's a miracle that you survived the crash, my love." Henrik takes a moment before he continues. "We will remember Sofie with the same warmth that flowed in her heart, as the remarkable person she was and, in a few hours, we will have the memorial so we can say our last farewells. Come now, my love, let's go over to the bridge." Joanna nods silently in agreement. Henrik gently wipes away the tears that remain on her cheeks with his hands before kissing. The kiss leaves a smooth and salty taste against his lips. The look she gives him makes the previously dark feeling in his heart go away altogether; they are a team, and each always feels the other in their heart.

With slow steps, Henrik gently pushes Joanna out of their quarters and they make their way up to the bridge. It's not a long walk but neither of them is in a hurry to reach the bridge. It too hard to say goodbye to their friend. Once they enter the bridge, they see pictures of Sofie placed all along the railing across the bridge, all the way down to the holoscreen at the very end. On the screen, a full-size hologram of Sofie rotates slowly, her arms crossed in an embrace and her eyes shut to signal that she rests now, her journey has ended. As they reach the very end of the bridge, they see that the entire crew has gathered below, awaiting and mourning the loss. Bjorn and Viterin stand in the front with their heads bowed down. Henrik takes a deep breath. He has read about the Zuoodi customs when it comes to the last goodbyes; they aren't too different from what he is used to back on Earth. But he has never before held a memorial service or a funeral for that matter.

With a low and calm tone, he begins.

"My friends and family, it's with a heavy heart we have gathered here today to say farewell to our Sofie, who we will always remember for her way of making the impossible possible." He takes a moment to recollect. As he looks across the mourning crew he comes to a decision, it's time to take a moment of silence.

"To honour Sofie, we shall now together take a moment of silence and remember her alive, full of spirit and energy." He bends his head down, letting the silence speak for itself for a moment. The only sound heard in the room is the crew's sobbing. A heavy atmosphere fills the room like a thunderstorm on a pitch-dark night. A feeling of loss and an endless void that Sofie leaves behind, felt by everyone on board. For most people, she was like a sister, a family member whom they had known for many years. The ceremony leaves no one untouched as the tears keep running. At the end of Henrik's speech, he gives the order to send out the black probe. A swooshing sound is heard throughout the bridge.

"With this probe, we will etch out an everlasting tribute to remember the sacrifice Sofie made to keep us all safe and to ensure our success," Henrik says.

The probe rushes towards the surface of the brown and grey asteroid. Using a mounted laser, it begins to etch a huge portrait of Sofie's face on the surface. The process is seen from the large glass panel on the front of the bridge. Henrik and the other patiently waits in silence while her face takes shape on the surface.

Part 34, Nauvis, new territory!

T he day after the ceremony, they land on
Nauvis, having received instructions on how
to proceed as they land. On the way down, they
had to navigate through a narrow canyon, leading
to what, with the naked eye, looks just like a
dead-end, a rock wall steeping high up. They
easily go through it and just slightly interfere with
the energy hologram. Thanks to Viterin's skilful
manoeuvring of the vessel, they safely land on the
other side.

Henrik stands in the lower deck with Joanna,
Anvu, and Bjorn awaiting the elevator to fully
extend down to the ground. They can hear metallic
sounds as the elevator pillars reach the ground. The
elevator pad begins to move. At first, Henrik sees
nothing, as for some reason it is quite dark outside
the ship. The air is heavy on the lungs and a metallic
taste reaches his mouth in an unpleasant manner.

"Let's hope that the taste of the air isn't the
norm on this planet," Henrik jokingly says. He is

dressed in his finest garment, a blue three-piece suit that his father once wore. This suit radiates confidence and at the same time shows respect for the older generals, who have kept the alliance alive for so long. It is decorated with golden seams on the shoulders swirling in different geometrical patterns, each pattern representing a part of the alliance.

When they come further down, they see that Yo-Kiel, together with a welcoming party, awaits them on the ground. Bjorn notices that Roukia is there as well, standing with several other high-ranking officers of the Alliance. As they reach the ground, a low-pitched rumble is heard. As they locate the direction from which the sound comes from, they see four enormous battleships that have triggered their thrusters at low power as a welcoming salutation. Not only is it heard, but it's also visually impressive as well. The thrusters light up the underground base with green and blue colours, like a firework firing downwards.

Yo-Kiel takes a few steps to the metallic grey elevator platform and greets them.

"It's a privilege to welcome you to Nauvis, Henrik, heir of Andromeda, Joanna, Anvu, and Bjorn." Yo-Kiel waves his hand in front of him as a gesture of respect, taking his downward-facing palm and turning it upwards to show that he isn't a threat; an old-fashioned yet still widely-used greeting, Henrik has been told. Yo-Kiel takes one more step forward as Henrik leaves the platform. With his right-hand outstretched, Yo-Kiel grabs Henrik's forearm just before the elbow begins. Henrik is quick to understand his intention and mirrors the movement, another courtesy greeting. Their grip on each other's forearms lasts only a short while as Yo-Kiel's face turns into a stern and serious expression when he takes a step backwards.

"I'm deeply sorry for your loss, our loss I must say. Sofie was an inspiring person who served the Alliance well." He ends the sentence with his head bowed downwards, "May she forever be remembered with grace." As he raises his head again, Yo-Kiel turns his attention towards Joanna. The stern face slowly turns into a great friendly smile, eyebrows slightly raised with joy and hands that once again dance in the air he said.

"And this must be the courageous and resource-ful Joanna we've heard so much about. The stories we have heard are impressive, to say the least." Joanna blinks in surprise. She wasn't aware that rumours about her part in the journey has spread so far.

With an equally joyful voice, she answers. "I feel flattered by your words, General. I must admit that

I wasn't aware that anyone has followed my actions during this journey." Joanna returns the dancing hand movement with an equally graceful gesture that ends with her palm facing upwards. Yo-Kiel's smile widens. He turns his greeting over to Anvu.

"Anvu! It has been ages since my eyes had the pleasure to meet yours, time has been kind towards you, welcome!" Anvu bows slightly forwards, she's been around long enough to recognize the difference between sincere kindness and kindness based on a hidden agenda. She has known of Yo-Kiel's infamous smooth-talking very well since her youth; he is sincere, to say the least. He was a good-looking guy back then, still is to her.

"Yo-Kiel, you silly old man," she says as they leave the platform.

Yo-Kiel points towards the four huge ships in the background. Henrik sees that people are moving all around on them, on the ground and all over the hull. Welding sparks can even be seen from this distance.

"The ship's colourful display that we showed you is only a fraction of their full power. This was and will once again be the pride and power centre of the Andromeda Alliance. This is the Nauvis Cloaked Shipyard." Pride is heard in his voice as he explains the cloaking hologram keeping them hidden. They move away from the platform and closer to the group.

Roukia shows her palm towards them as they come closer and so does everyone else in the group. Together they form the downwards pointing arrow sign with their hands as a display of loyalty. Henrik does the same and Joanna is quick to repeat the sign. Roukia is dressed in a black robe.

Henrik feels an unnerving feeling that something isn't right. He doesn't know why, so he shakes away the feeling for now. *Something is off, dig deeper*, he thinks, making a mental note of the surroundings.

"Welcome my friends, welcome to the Alliance," Roukia says, her robe gently moving as she talks. Her eyes travel from Henrik to Bjorn and land on Joanna's.

"Let me introduce myself, Joanna, we haven't met before, but I have heard a lot about you, I am Roukia. I served with Henrik's father and now I serve under our new leader towards the freedom of the galaxy." Her voice is short and precise, the perfect voice for an senior, disciplined general, Joanna thinks. One by one they all introduce themselves, the elite of the Alliance. Generals and faction leaders from the old and several younger faces are seen in the background. One face catches her eyes, a young boy who is strikingly like Henrik, even with the same slightly crooked nose that he had when he was younger. Must be a coincidence, she assumes, putting the thought aside.

When they have greeted one another, Yo-Kiel waves for a very handsome gentleman dressed in a black turtleneck jumper to come forward. Henrik finds that the jumper makes the person look as sophisticated and cultured as a person can ever look. On the left side of the jumper a symbol is placed a black arrow. Henrik notices that it is only visible when the light comes from the right angle; otherwise, it blends in with the fabric. Yo-Kiel introduces him as the Commander of the fleet and chief mechanic.

"Henrik Harlacker, it is an honour to meet you, let me introduce myself further." He places his hand on the arrow, which begins to glow. Shortly after, the entire base room is lit up from above. The massive base extends beyond what can be seen with the naked eye. Buildings and scaffolding almost blend in with the large ships. Glowing chips from angle grinders and flames from welds are seen from all directions around the ships. Large, old cranes lift material to assembly points on the hulls of the different ships.

"The work is intense here," Henrik says. the man turns around as he answers.

"It truly is Henrik, it truly is."

"Impressive way to introduce yourself, Commander. What's your name?" Henrik asks, the man in front of them smiles.

"Thank you, that was the reaction I was hoping to get. My name is Evan. Up until you arrived, I was the Commander of the fleet and the chief mechanic," Evan says, pausing briefly before continuing. "It is my privilege to hand over the title to our true leader and Commander in Chief." He removes the symbol from his jumper and hands it over to Henrik. With his right hand, Henrik secures the arrow on his suit.

"Nice to meet you, Evan. I saw a large workforce on the ships; it would be interesting to see more of how you work around here."

"It would be my pleasure. I know the vessels like the back of my hand," Evan answers. "Come follow me and let me give you a brief tour around the fleet." He begins to walk towards the ships as Henrik and the other follow. From the buildings ahead of them, a network of conveyor belts without railings spreads in the direction of the ships. People are seen travelling at rapid speeds to and from the shipyard. At junctions, you simply shift between the different bands to get there quickly. As soon as they come near the first ship, Evan describes the intricate details

"Since we first heard that you arrived, we've been

working day and night to prepare the ships for your return." Evan makes a pause as he effortlessly jumps off the belt; they have arrived at the first ship. Henrik is quick to follow, but unfortunately, he is not as smooth and elegant, so six short and quick stumbling steps later he also stands still. Henrik thinks the ship in front of them must be at least five hundred meters long or more. It's a huge piece of machinery. Coated in a dark grey painting, he notices that it has seen some action during its life, as a patchwork of metal sheets cover some areas that have previously been damaged. Along the side, a burn mark is etched. Evan activates a holographic display near them. The ship is seen in a blue hue.

"Here you have one of our three Kylo-class ships. Since it's one of our oldest vessels it is named *Genesis*; Yo-Kiel is captain over it. It's a heavy cruiser equipped with massive firepower. It holds nearly a thousand drones that can be sent out like bees from their hive. The drones themselves are powered by a highly intelligent AI that constantly undergoes new scenarios and learns the enemy's weaknesses." Evan turns around and points towards two adjacent ships, similar in style but they look wider and heavier somehow.

"And over there you see the other two Kylo-class ships, which are equipped with more firepower than the one beside us. Both have roughly the same number of combat drones, we call them *Kalypso* and *Kuno*. Only *Kuno* has a captain at the moment," Evan says.

Henrik's eye catches four abnormally large, elongated structures going from each side of one of the ships. Each one is pointing forward and slightly outward at different angles.

"What are those structures on the ship, thrusters?" Henrik asks. Evan smiles as he hoped that questions soon would come. He uses the holodisplay to highlight the structures so everyone can see.

"Of course, Commander, as you can see on the display, the structures are in fact four heavy pulse cannons, capable of massive destruction," Evan says, taking a short break, letting everyone focus on the display for a second. When he thinks that they have seen enough, he starts showing on the display how the cannon works. "The pulse that is fired is massive and produced through an internal and complex particle accelerator inside the hull of the ship, taking heavy particles into a closed-loop torus chamber in order to accumulate the particles, until it's time for discharge."

At the base of the cannon, Henrik can see a red pulsating light in what he guesses is the closed-loop chamber. As the cannon fires, the light quickly accelerates along with the cannon and out.

"The output is surprisingly large for its size. It's peak Joule at impact is 0.9 Tera Joules, if converted to Earth standards," Evan explains. Bjorn and Henrik look at each other in amazement. The numbers are too big to even think about what kind of damage the weapon is capable of. He folds and puts away the portable display into his pocket.

"Besides the larger cannons, the ships are equipped with point defence cannons, fifteen on each side, capable of very rapid and unforgiving accuracy. They're bit like your pulse gun but with more energy and rapid-fire. They are good for taking down drones or smaller ships, the aiming and firing is all done by AI of course," Evan concludes.

He continues to briefly discuss the reason why AI controls the actual firing of the weapons while they take a short journey further down the belt. They reach an even larger, enormous ship, unlike the others. It's dark blue, with a frame that curves in a raindrop shape around the ship's hull, making it appear even larger.

It's unnecessarily aerodynamically shaped, Henrik thinks. In the middle of the frame, the ship's hull begins. As with the core of an avocado, the hull sits inside.

"Besides the unusual design, the purpose of the

ship is obvious," Evan says, though it is obvious that neither Henrik, Joanna, nor Bjorn can see it.

"I'm sorry Evan, what is the purpose of this strange ship?" Joanna asks, her eyes are fixed on the strange avocado shaped frame.

"This is our pride and glory, we call her SSA *Kraken*, or Space Ship Andromeda the Kraken, equipped with pulse cannons on each side, in sets of two, and missile tubes all along the hull," he pauses for a second, letting them take in the name. "She is made for one purpose, and one purpose only: eliminating an enemy ship with one single shot, while holding massive firepower to subdue enemy ships and drones." With his arms he follows the frame, making sure the others see his movements.

"As the energy accumulates inside the hull, the entire structure glows deep purple. The energy is led from the centre of the hull to the frame and out in an impressively powerful and spectacular concentrated beam. The beam keeps its radius over a huge distance with only minor bleeding or loss of focus." Evan picks up the holoscreen from his pocket, where immediately they can see an animation. The large ship is in the centre of a formation, the three smaller Kylo ships together with a swarm of hundreds of drones to protect SSA *Kraken*. "When in combat, the mission of Kraken is to eliminate the enemy leader with precision. One flaw in the design is that when the shot is fired, the shields become inoperative for a split second due to the energy release, so timing is of utmost importance" Evan says.

The animation shows a shot being fired against an enemy ship. With brute power and a badly edited animation, the enemy ship is torn in two. Sparks are seen from the entry hole of the beam, any matter that the beam passed through is completely vaporized. Nothing but empty space is left. The animation fades out. Henrik clears his throat loudly, putting his right fist towards his mouth before commenting on what he just saw.

"Evan, my friend, the enormous power that this vessel gives us will certainly secure our victory when we take back Andromeda." He points towards the other ships with his arms. "I see a lot of people working on the ships. How soon can the fleet be ready?"

Evan brings out another device from one of his inner pockets. "Let me just catch up on the progress for today." He rapidly scrolls through a list on his device. "Ah yes, I see," he mumbles to himself, "Okay if we include today's progress, we are following the plan perfectly. That rarely happens but we have great engineers and technicians here on Nauvis," he proudly says as he puts back the device into his inner pocket.

"So, to answer your question Henrik, the fleet will be ready in around two years if we stay on track," Evan says. Henrik nods as a reply; he's pleased with the answer.

Part 35, Telling tales of glory!

H enrik finds himself struggling to cope with the mere scale of the operation after seeing the huge ships. They travel back along the belt. It is eye-opening for him as he realizes not only how large the scale of battle will be, but also, how monumental the cost will be to be free them from the tyranny that Tidus has over the system.

Will we even survive the coming battle? What will be left? he thinks. He grabs Joanna's hand as they leave the belt. They have arrived back to where they started, near where they landed.

"I hope the tour was of satisfaction for you all," Evan says. There is something on his foot that catches Henrik's eyes. A loose cable hangs out of his pants and down against his shoes.

"Nothing to worry about, it's just a wire. I'll fix it later when I get back to my quarters." He tries to brush off what they saw and distract them. "Let me lead you to the party, there is much to be done, and much to be seen." He points towards a large metallic building a few hundred meters away.

"Lead the way, Evan. We are ready."

When they enter the building, they are greeted by a loud applause. They have just walked in on a large stage inside the building hall. In front of them around round tables, several hundred people are waiting for them. Henrik walks up to a podium and stands proudly on the stage, showing the people in front of him the arrow greeting with his hands pointing down. He takes Joanna's hand and holds it tenderly and proudly. The applause continues and slowly turns into a rhythmic melody before it gradually subsides. The crowd is now silent, waiting for what will happen.

"I didn't know what to expect when I entered this building. To see you all applauding for our arrival truly warms my heart," Henrik says, his voice is amplified and heard from speakers around the hall. "It will be my pleasure to get to know each and every one of you, to show you who we are and what we can do for you." He takes a sip from a glass that was out on the podium. The crowd listens closely for his next words. "I will keep this speech short, because will have plenty of time to discuss all important matters later, my friends. Let me just say that I am very impressed by you all, keeping the Alliance alive and ready for new glory!" The crowd applauds his words.

"We have seen Tidus' cruel and oppressive rule of Zuood, how the people suffer terribly and how they together with Youllian forces uphold the oppression. How the streets are filled with guards taking every opportunity to humiliate and punish the people of Zuood!" The silence is deafening. "I say, no more! Enough is enough!" Henrik lifts his fists in the air, creating momentum for the crowd. They are quick to react and roar in approval, a fast and rhythmic applaud fills the hall with energy Henrik has never seen before. It only ends as they have left the stage, moved to the seating area, and the performance artist begins to dance.

"That was an impressive speech you made, my friend," Bjorn says, standing near the tables below the stage with a glass of wine in his hand. "Now, let's enjoy the party and have a great time, we deserve it."

"Sounds like a plan, my friend, but there is something I must do first." Henrik sees that Yo-Kiel is sitting a few tables away, and he signals him to move over to them.

"Hi, enjoying the party, are we?" he asks while Yo-Kiel takes a seat. The general raises his glass.

"Greetings Henrik and Joanna, I am honoured to be by your side at the table."

Henrik's curiosity must be saturated; he wonders what strengths they will encounter once they meet Tidus. He takes a sip from his glass before asking.

"What do we know about Tidus' fleet, and what can we expect? What are his strengths, weaknesses?" Unprepared for the direct question, Yo-Kiel also takes a sip and puts down his glass again before answering.

"What our scouts have found is that Tidus' ships are heavily armed and equipped with the very latest technology. They have several large motherships that include thousands of drones and battleships with powerful cannons and energetic rail guns." He takes another sip to moisten his throat, holding the glass in the air while he continues. "However, we lack information about Youllian forces, but we have received confirmation that due to very poor resources and routines around the management of the fleet, not many of the larger ships are in operation now." Yo-Kiel puts the glass down on the table. Henrik picks up his glass as a thank you, but his question is not yet fully answered, he thinks.

"I understand, but what can we expect to face in battle?" Henrik says, leaning against the table.

"We will face strong opposition, no doubt, but we will also have the upper hand to some extent if we succeed in firing *Kraken* against Tidus' main ship. If we take it, we have won. However, I sincerely hope that we will be able to complete our ships before it's time." He puts down the glass. "Without a fully functioning ship, the battle will be even more difficult than we can imagine. Our crew is very capable, but that is not enough," Yo-Kiel looks down at the glass, which is now almost empty. "I will be more than happy to discuss our battle plan further Henrik, whenever you want, but let's now return to the party. It's time for joy and celebration, not for planning." Henrik agrees and takes out the carafe that is closest, filling both glasses.

The party is gaining momentum and more artists are performing on stage. Between the performances, a few generals give speeches. Among them, a general stands out from the rest. She is dressed in a black robe and her appearance on stage stirred up the participants in the party. Sudden outbursts of booing or clapping come from different tables.

"Who is that?" Joanna asks Bjorn.

"Didn't think that she had the guts to appear on stage, my friend. That is Quintion. For some reason she believes herself to be the rightful leader over the Alliance," Bjorn answers with hatred in his voice.

"I see, tell us more," she says.

"In the past, she has tried to convince other generals to take over the leadership, unsuccessfully of course, but she takes every opportunity to spread rumours and polarize the political landscape."

As Quintion begins her speech, Bjorn continues.

"Her full name is Quintion of Aheulu. She is the daughter of Matu's former right-hand man Yson, who died during the war. Yson sacrificed his life as he protected Matu so that he could reach Henrik and send his son to Earth. I guess she never accepted it."

"I see, does her belief have followers among the public?" Joanna asks.

"Not really. She is despised by the public as she had made some dubious decisions and claims before, trying to smear Matu's legacy and leadership without anything to back it up." A combination of booing and clapping is heard again from the surrounding tables. "However, some generals are leaning towards what she said; she isn't shy when it comes to giving empty promises to weak generals who wish to climb their ladder."

Henrik, who has listened to their conversation, jumps in.

"Keep her under surveillance and give me a list of the supporting generals. I wish to have as much information as possible about her claims so we can prove her wrong and end her attempt to polarize our people."

If there is something Henrik despises, it is cowards attempt to exploit people's fears in order to gain power.

"Of course, Henrik, will do," Bjorn answers.

Part 36, The sound of thunder!

A few weeks has passed when Henrik suddenly wakes up from his slumber. He has barely had time to sleep during the night. He was disturbed by a loud noise, howling like a siren outside their room, which wouldn't let him sleep. As he opens his eyes, he sees that the wall mouldings in the room flash rhythmically brightly red. The sound reminds him of the warning of an air attack back on Earth. Before Henrik even has had time to blink, Joanna is already on her feet.

"Come on, you know what this sound means, get up!" She commands him and tosses his clothes onto the bed. Henrik takes his right hand and gives himself a hard slap on his face to wake up; it works.

"I'm on it, let's move!" With rapid hands he pulls the dark blue pants back on, snaps the buttons of his shirt, and throws on the heavy, ornate jacket. With a smooth movement, he jumps into his shoes.

They move together as one towards the door.

"A year has passed since we came to the base, my love. We have trained for this," Joanna shouts as she feels how her heart pounds beneath her blouse. "The siren can only mean one thing. We are discovered." Her words echo through Henrik's mind.

They move quickly towards the command centre, which is located down the hall outside their room. When they reach the door, they stop for a second to collect themselves. As the door opens smoothly with a swishing sound, they see that they are not the first ones to arrive. Yo-Kiel and Bjorn stand next to their respective chairs around a large table in the middle of the room. Staring at the screen in front of them, Henrik and Joanna both take their seats around the table, carefully watching a briefing on the holographic screen.

"The three dots on the screen represents the intruders," Bjorn explains. As they watch how the ships entered the base just minutes ago Bjorn describes the scene. "We have been infiltrated and found; I believe that it's Chronos scouts that have infiltrated our base. Two of them turned around and made the daring attempt of jumping into hyperspace while still in the planet's atmosphere." Two of the dots disappear. "One succeeded and the other was obliterated into small pieces as it was hit mid-jump by the energy from a pulse cannon." They closely follow everything that happens on the screen, "The third ship was able to vanish somewhere between the Kylo ships. They probably already jumped out and walk amongst us by now." Bjorn's face reveals a very agitated man who isn't all that amused to being disturbed in the middle of the night by a couple of intruders. With a calm and focused voice, Joanna directs her thoughts towards the vanished scout ship.

"I see, Bjorn. There must have been someone who saw something. We have people working day and night in order to get the ships ready." She thumbs on the desk impatiently as she goes through in her head what outcome this intrusion brings. This past year she has climbed the ladder and taken a high position as captain and leader of the first Kylo ship.

"We have no reports of any sighting, but we have sent out a search and secure team who will locate the infiltrator sooner or later," Bjorn says as he brings up more details on the screen.

"We were able to crack the identity of the ship that vanished. We have confirmed through the ledger that the ships are indeed Chronos in origin." The ships' names and hashes are seen on the display. "This intrusion can only mean one thing. Tidus' fleet is already on their way towards us." Bjorn sighs. "we have to get all out of here and into position outside of orbit." He looks towards Henrik.

Henrik strokes his now long, full beard with his right hand, a habit he has acquired when he considers different possibilities. Other generals and captains have entered the room now, closely following every move he makes. Henrik stands up, ready to speak, to give his intentions and orders.

"One thing is sure, the time has come for us to be brave now, braver than we probably have ever been before in our lives; we must face the corporation head-on or take the consequences that come when doing nothing," Henrik takes a moment to let his words settle before he continues.

"We know now that Tidus have our location and that he will be here shortly with his full force against us. We are probably outnumbered, but together with your crews, the ships we have are a deadly force that will rupture Tidus' entire galaxy to its foundation!" His short speech doesn't give the reaction he was hoping for. Instead of an energized, hyped crowd, he finds that the generals are mostly silent. A few of them talk with muffled voices amongst themselves; no individual words can be perceived. Henrik can feel the dissatisfaction and anxiety in the crowd, he just isn't sure why they are reacting in this way. Henrik's eyes are looking for an answer, so he turns to Joanna to find support. She is outright furious at their reaction. He sees that her fist is clenched, she struggles to contain herself.

One general, a woman dressed in a red and black robe, takes a step forward. The other generals fall silent.

"I have to speak up and give the opinion of my fellow generals. The fleet is far from ready to go all in and face the wrath of Tidus' entire fleet!" The others back her up with nodding heads and agreeing voices. At first, Henrik doesn't recognize her; she had different clothing at the party but now he remembers her voice *I know who you are, don't you for a second believe that you will accomplish your goal of taking over today, or any day for that matter*, Henrik thinks as he signals her to continue.

"Then speak up and explain to us what you find challenging? Quintion of Aheulu, yes I do know who you are and yes I am aware of your intentions," Henrik says. Her facial expressions reveal her dislike. After taking a few seconds to put her anger aside, she continues.

"What do we know of Tidus' fleet now, a year later? How can you demand that we take the fight without even knowing what we will face out there? I believe that if we move now we are doomed to fail.

We will be obliterated and forgotten." Quintion takes one more step forward, raising her voice to invoke a reaction from her supporters, "This time, I will allow myself to be completely shameless. I want us all to recognize your failure as our leader. Who are you even? Why should we follow you? Your leadership will be our death!" Her last word makes the generals behind her take a step back. She went too far, and she knows it. Meanwhile, Joanna struggles to maintain her anger inside.

How dare they behave like insecure, whispering, impatient and cowardly leaders, she wonders. *They hear that the whole base is threatened, and their reaction is to distrust Henrik? They will hear a word of truth!* Joanna abruptly rises from her chair; she hits her fist hard on the table as she starts scolding them.

"This has to end right now! Don't you see what she is trying to do; she tries to take the focus away from the only current issue in the room: the threat to our existence! The fight before us will not be easy or without losses, but everything we stand for, and everyone we fight for, is determined by the outcome of this fight!" Joanna takes a short break to catch her breath. With a slightly calmer tone she says, "Now I tell you that the time has come to show your support and courage in this difficult time. Will you do it? Or are you going to listen to the imitator who has shown no qualitative characteristics as a leader. She has only sought to undermine Henrik's leadership, without revealing her own ideas and solutions. Make your choice, and make it now!" Her voice echoes in everyone's ears. A slow clapping sound comes from a few of the generals. Her words have been heard. Quintion stands with drooping shoulders as she realizes she has lost the argument.

"See you up there, our fate and doom are in your hands. Henrik, I'll prepare my station," she says before turning around to leave the room. No one is looking in her direction.

"What I hope you all take with you from this discussion is that the most important thing of all right now is that we act as a united front against Tidus! We stand as one or fall as one! Our intel regarding the Tidus fleet will be shared with you all. Now I ask you to prepare your team for battle, for a battle is what we inevitably have before us, my friends!" Henrik says, knowing that the last struggle with Quintion is yet to be won.

There will come a time when I have to deal with her once and for all. Henrik gives the floor to Bjorn, who signals that something new has arrived through the com.

"If the drama is over now, I hope you all can move

your attention to the new intel that just arrived. The search team reports that they have captured the intruder now and put him under arrest, and more importantly, we have received a message from one of our field agents," Bjorn says. On the screen, a short message containing only eleven words are seen.

Tidu's fleet is gathering just outside of Zuood. Prepare yourself. Kilo.

"As you all can see, this message confirms what we already believed to be true, our scout with the codename Kilo makes this crystal clear, it is now or never!" Henrik says.

Part 37, Into oblivion!

Morning has turned into day and into late evening again as all the preparations for lift-off have been completed. Henrik is seated in the captain's seat inside the *Kraken* mothership. The seat is wide; he finds that the new bridge environment inside *Kraken* fits him very well. The room is about the same size as it was in *Eclipse*, maybe somewhat smaller, but the whole atmosphere seems to be designed to give a sense of urgency.

On the floor, a pulsating light pattern shimmers in green and blue in a slow rhythm, the walls have octagonal shapes that go from the floor all the way to the roof. Crew members are either standing or sitting behind large holopanels. Henrik can see eight stations from his chair. He witnesses on the holoscreen in front of him how the *Kuno*, the last ship to declare itself ready for liftoff, signals green for liftoff. A smile on his face reveals his anticipation. They are almost ready now. Both

Bjorn and Evan are seated opposite Henrik, their chairs placed slightly off-centre so that they give a straight line of sight for the captain to have an overview of the bridge.

"Today has been hectic, but I'm more than satisfied with the impressive quickness with which the different crews have prepared the ships ready for lift-off," Henrik says. Bjorn nods and notices how Henrik has changed clothes, from the decorated official dark blue jacket into a more versatile outfit, a black shirt with the arms cuffed up.

"This is it, my friends. This is what has been brewing in the background all of our lives." Bjorn says with pride in his heart.

"I can feel it too, my friend. As you know, the plan is to enter a formation a quarter-million kilometres away from the planet, interlocking into each other's hyperdrives to make a synchronous jump." Henrik displays the movements on the screen. As the ships slowly align, he continues, "This will take us to the edge of Zuood's system. Hopefully, our sudden movement will surprise Tidus' forces, giving us the advantage we need." He pauses the visualization of the ships as a call comes from *Kalypso*, the first Kylo ship that Joanna is the captain on. It tells them that it's almost time for liftoff. On the screen, a three-dimensional image of her head appears.

"Joanna to *Kraken*. With General Yo-Kiel's *Genesis* ship ready, all ships have declared ready to go. Only minutes left now until *Kuno* as the first ship takes to the sky," she says. Henrik notices the smile on her face as she almost jumps with excitement. *It's nice to see her like this*, he thinks. With his hand in the air, he gestures to Bjorn and Evan to let them have a private conversation. They get the point and leave their chairs empty.

"Thank you, Captain Joanna, that is good news. Our ship is just behind yours so we will lift directly after you. See you up there, my love," he answers. Her smile brightens even more. "And remember, I am very proud of you. Whatever happens in our near future; remember." Joanna nods as a thank you.

"You are everyone's inspiration and hope at this moment, my dear, we will come through this together and we will win!" she says, giving him a kiss in the air before she ends the call.

A few minutes later, a tremendous thunder rumbles in front of *Kraken* as *Kalypso* leaves the base. She leaves a dust cloud inside the base so heavy in the air that normal visibility is all lost. Henrik is prepared to leave the base as soon as the Kylo ships in front of them have left the ground.

"Give me a full report of the ship's sensor status,

Davood," Henrik says as they prepare the last steps in the checklist before they can take to the sky. Davood manipulates a screen in front of him with ease; the new interface in the *Kraken* is more intuitive.

"Sensors shows no unusual readings, hull integrity is at one hundred per cent, boosters are ready, all communications bandwidths are open." Davood turns around, facing Henrik. "As the reparation work was interrupted by the intruders, we are now compensating auxiliary power from the lower decks."

"Thank you, Davood, we will have to make it with the energy that we have. Once we are in high system orbit, we'll need to charge the tachyon field capacitors. Do we have enough power for that still?"

"We have more than enough for the jump and to recover through the hyperspace with almost full shield capacity," Davood said.

"Great, then let's get this bird of the planet and join the others in orbit," Henrik commands.

Once in orbit, the ships align, combining their tachyon fields, charging the negative matter compensators until the target level is reached. The chargeback from the jump shakes loose items inside the ships as they enter hyperspace

"The trip will only take a few minutes, as we now

have combined capacity," Davood reports.

Henrik activates the com channel fleet-wide. "This is it, my friends, this is what you are fighting for. In a few minutes, we will take the fight directly to Tidus. You are ready!"

Part 38, Tidus!

T he walls of the battleship *Exitium*'s bridge have light, smooth, and slightly marble-like walls. The walls are covered in an abundance of golden details from the decorative mouldings to the bridge crew's consoles. *Exitium* is Chronos Corporations heaviest battleship. The ship has an armament of pulse energy cannons on each side of the hull, distributed in eight sections per side, four cannons per section: a considerable penetration force. This, combined with hundreds of drones gives the ship an almost unbeatable strength, Tidus is very aware and proud of this.

Tidus himself stands proud on the bridge; his straight posture and chiselled jaw reveal a muscular body. A black metallic muscle cuirass is snuggly fitted on his body to enhance his appearance even more. In front of him, he has his soon-to-be-retired Youllian leader Zuth, discussing how to deal with the newfound intel they received from their scouts. An urgent message on the holoscreen attracts their attention.

Sensors have detected an unknown energy signature outside the system, distance four point three Astronomical Units. Time of Detection to Statement is thirty-two minutes.

Tidus raises his narrow eyebrows in surprise as he reads it for a second time.

Could it be them?" he wonders. *No, they would never dare to make such a bold move, taking the fight directly to us?*

Zuth is fast on his hands and opens the sensory display log, carefully looking at the energy signatures to determine what it can be. As he is sure of what he's looking at, he faces Tidus, whose eyes are filled with malicious thoughts. Before Zuth has the chance to speak, with a low and calm voice Tidus says, "So, it begins."

On the screen, the energy signatures remain as they are.

"Instruct the other ships that we are on red alert and take us to the edge of the system. We will let the Alliance know that they are no match for our forces," Tidus says. Zuth immediately obeys. As his hands manipulate the screen's controls, he remembers that a Youllian battle convoy stationed in a nearby system can come and aid them on short notice.

"I must advise you to call in our secondary forces. We are yet to understand what we will meet," Zuth says, making sure to be as neutral as possible not to agitate Tidus in any way. He is well aware of the man's short temper and impulsive manner.

"No need to bother them. Before they can arrive, this whole thing will be over. Remember our secret weapon, Zuth? We control this system in more ways than the Alliance even can fathom with their small minds. Remember our hidden resources," Tidus says, referring to several hidden military bases located at strategic points around the system. Zuth stays quiet; he is in no mood to risk anything today of all days, the last day in active duty before his retirement.

In addition to *Exitium*, the fleet consists of two attack vessels capable of medium to short-range pulse bursts. They are sleek and painted dark grey. On all sides of the ship, extendable pulse, rail guns sweep back and forth searching for a target. Alongside the attack vessels, there is one heavy cruiser for long-range defence. The ship is just a drone's length away from stretching a thousand meters in length. Each side of the ship is comprised of several drone hangar bays, with a capacity of hundreds of drones at one time, and the long-range pulse cannons combined with Gatling turrets makes it a formidable defensive wall of steel and firepower.

Zuth longs for his rather old but trusted cruiser. He decides he will take it for one last trip when this is all over, a trip to the outer edges of the system. There, on a small and less populated planet, he will retire for good. But for now, Zuth can only obey, to once again in his lifetime be forced into obeying the pulsating bright red light that makes the crew aware of the impending battle. He watches in awe as crewmembers move all around the ships in preparation.

The ships use their side thrusters to rearrange their heading before they engage their main thrusters as the vessels align themself towards the correct trajectory.

"As soon as we are within range, send out the primary drones first, then go in with the attack vessels, and focus the cannons on the weak points of the ships. Use the hidden bases to fire from their rear side, fire in bursts of four at a time until they are paralyzed, let's make this fight quick and dirty. Henrik the 'heir' isn't worth my time. Neither was his weak father," Tidus says as he lets out a short laugh.

The laugh makes Zuth feel chills down his spine,

yet he nods in silence as to confirm that he heard the order, he is tired. Tidus looks out through the bridge's holographic screen, showing the view from the outside. He sees how four ships are on the way towards them from the outer edge of the system. They are so far away that he needs to zoom in on them, but Tidus knows that the battle will soon begin.

"You will see, soon you will be just a memory. Your alliance has not existed for many years now," says Tidus aloud to himself.

Part 39, The fight!

W hen they reach a point just outside of the system, Henrik orders all ships to reverse their thrusters.

"We make our stand here! Prepare formation, you know what to do, my captains," he says as the shadow of Zuood's sister planet Zooul touches the bridge area. The four ships de-accelerate until they reach just above outer system orbit speed, slowly racing towards the anticipated position of Tidus' fleet. Henrik has knowingly chosen this position as an attempt to keep debris from colliding with the inner inhabited planets to a minimum.

Bjorn is standing next to a control panel watching how the enemy ships begin their advance.

"Tidus' forces push forward and will soon be within range, Henrik. They're at a distance of four-point one AU and closing in fast," Bjorn reports. Henrik glances on the control panels, waiting in silence for the moment that shall come.

"Ready the drones, send all of them out at once.

From what I have read from Tidus' previous battle history, we need to make sure that the enemy drones are eliminated as soon as possible," Henrik says.

Bjorn forwards the order, even though he does not feel confident in the chosen tactics. He believes that the drones will not damage Tidus' ship but will just prolong the battle, increasing the losses and jeopardizing the entire battle. He has previously pointed this out, although he recognizes that the charge time for Kraken's primary beam weapon is time-sensitive.

"Time will tell if this is the right move, my friend," he almost whispers.

"It sure will," Henrik replies.

The distance between the two fleets decreases at a rapid pace. *Exitium* and Tidus' fleet mirror Henrik's ships movements a couple of minutes after their initial flanking positions, the time it takes for the sensors to report calculated distance and position decreases the closer the fleets move to each other.

Their velocity is steady. Henrik knows that there are only two possible outcomes of this battle, and the crew members of the fleet do as well. They are tense; war is upon them. Henrik feels confident in the strategy they have devised in a relatively short time. He knows that the crew is more than ready for this. Some of them have trained since a young age. With this in his mind, Henrik realizes that the battle is not his. This battle is the crew's and the crew's only. He only leads them into a hopeful future, but this is their struggle for freedom, for a life without totalitarian rule. He activates the com channel fleet wide once more.

"This is the commander speaking." He gives them a few seconds before he continues. "For better or for worse, this is the day when everything will be decided. Will we live free and form a true alliance once more? Or will we die trying?"

Their response took him by surprise as a roar from his crew echoes on the bridge and throughout the fleet. Their fists clenched in the air while they shout their battle cry, filled with adrenaline, anxiety, and hope all mixed together. He reckons that they are ready. Glancing out over the bridge, Henrik's eyes wander with a sense of pride in his heart in how his crew keep a close eye on everything that the ship's sensors report. From one screen to another, they have an overview of everything that happens, following the analysed and calculated position of Chronos' ships.

"*Kalypso* to *Kraken*, we are ready to send out our drones, just give the command," Joanna reports. Henrik notices on the screen how her facial expression, usually so smooth and calm, is replaced. Her eyebrows and a tiny crinkle on her forehead reveal her level of focus.

"Captain Joanna, send them away with maximum velocity when we reach a distance of point double zero six AU and let them wreak havoc on the enemy drones until we reach the point of intersection," he answers. The first encounter with Tidus' fleet is only minutes away now.

"Affirmative, launching all available drones at that distance, over and out," she replies. Knowing that the words she is speaking at this moment might be the last words they share if anything goes wrong, her stomach aches.

As the fleet reaches firing distance, a series of events unfolds in front of Henrik. Looking out through the primary display, he sees how the drone tubes run hot. Drone after drone exits the ships like how a wasp swarm leaves their hive to protect against intruders.

Kraken's pulse cannon turrets rotate out from the hull, firing its dual barrels relentlessly towards the oncoming fleet ahead in bursts of four. Metal sections open around the hull, exposing missile tubes ready to launch deadly micro nukes. The ships are now in the visible range of each other, de-accelerating.

"Chronos vessel locking weapons on us, sir"

"Evan, evasive pattern Z nine, make it difficult for them," Henrik orders, knowing that evasive pattern might lower the amount of damage they will take just a fraction, but every little advantage is vital.

"Acknowledged," Evan replies, adjusting the flight pattern in an upwards angle.

In what felt like seconds, the space between the fleets is filled with drones, projectiles, blasts, and carnage. Henrik sees how energy signatures behind them suddenly appear on the screen. Several hundred projectiles heading towards them follow shortly.

"Evan!"

"I see them, Commander, directing focus." Evan concentrates the heavy armaments on the port side of the ship to fire against the oncoming projectiles.

"They are targeting *Genesis*; we can't isolate individual robots," Bjorn reports.

Henrik sees how the ship Yo-Kiel captains receives hit after hit. The ship's cannons fire rapidly in an attempt to fight off the incoming missiles.

"Primary shields are down to thirteen per cent. The hull has been breached on several non-shielded sections, not sure on how much more of this we can..." Yo-Kiel disappears from the com as a blast critically impacts the hull, the carnage is total.

It feels like the air is sucked right out of his chest as Henrik sees how *Genesis* splits into two pieces drifting away from each other. Nothing could have prepared him for the grim battle scene.

"Goodbye, my friend," is all that Henrik manages to say, a farewell towards a ruptured heart.

Suddenly he feels a large hand heavily on his shoulder.

"Now is not the time to be paralyzed, we will mourn our friend after we have won the battle, my friend." Bjorn says as he shakes Henrik into focus.

Henrik's lungs fill with air as he straightens his back, his heart still heavy from the sudden loss. The world around him returns. Voices fill the entire bridge. In the middle of the noise, he hears that the drones are starting to decrease in number. The missiles that shot down *Genesis* focus on both remaining ships. A sense of desperation begins to spread throughout the crew. Henrik presses the fleet com radio button.

"This is your commander speaking. Fight for all that is worth fighting for. Fight like the faith of the entire galaxy hangs on your shoulders. Fight!"

A wild roar echoes from every section of both ships. The second phase of the battle is upon them. On the screen he sees that at the same time as Joanna's ship is taking heavy damage, *Kraken*'s main weapon is almost fully charged, he needs a distraction, he needs it quickly.

"The drones!" he shouts.

"Send all drones towards the incoming missiles. The debris might hinder further projectiles from passing through," Henrik says, sending the order forward to Evan who controls the drones' flight pattern. Within moments, the drones scatter from the main battle between the fleets and heads straight towards the incoming missiles.

"This might just work," he reflects as he follows everything from the bridge. They still take damage on non-shielded sections of the ship and the impacts are felt throughout the entire structure, the walls echo of metal clashing into each other.

"Do we have confirmed the identity of Tidus' ship?" he asks Bjorn.

"We have analysed the communication pattern of the enemy fleet and we are almost certain that Tidus commands from the largest of the ships. We first thought that it was a decoy, but now we are certain. Tidus is present at the ship called *Exitium*," Bjorn answers.

"Fire the *Kraken*'s main weapon directly at that ship as soon as fully charged," Henrik says. His mind is set for victory.

Part 40, Tidus last breath!

As Tidus watches how the Alliance's drones suddenly retreat to the fleet, he feels that he can't fully comprehend what the motive is, he laughs to himself.

"Do you see that, Zuth? They think that they can win by sacrificing a few drones, pathetic!" he says.

"I see, my commander," he answers without much energy. All he longs for is the stillness of retirement or death.

Tidus' lips form a thin smile when he thinks about how to crush the Alliance with one last decisive push forward.

"They do believe that they are something, I must say. They are either very bold, stupid, or perhaps both. Let's finish this now once and for all." He points towards Zuth, "Take us closer, we will crush them like the ants that they are, send in one of the attack vessels for full ramming speed," Tidus says.

Zuth raises his eyebrows out of Tidus' sight as he forwards the command down the line. Within seconds, the fleet's main thrusters ignite and they move closer. Zuth has a hard time understanding who Tidus intends to sacrifice, as the attack ship is likely to be destroyed in the collision. But he knows better than to make the slightest comment about it.

"Full ramming speed I said, didn't I?" Tidus says as he notices that the attack vessel hasn't activated all thrusters. He is more than annoyed at this.

"My apologies, Commander, I'll make sure that they comply. Which ship should they ram?" Zuth asks.

"Take the smaller vessel. I trust that Henrik lurks inside the larger. I want him alive after all," Tidus says. He elevates his jaw and with his hands behind his back, he watches how the ship is sent away towards its destiny.

A few minutes pass by. The two fleets are hammering each other with pulse after pulse. Projectiles rattle into already-damaged hull parts to inflict further damage. The area between the fleets is filled with debris from destroyed drones from both sides. With his hands still snug behind his back, Tidus watches with contentment how the battle evolves around him. In his mind, it's a beautiful dance of carnage and destruction.

On *Kraken*'s bridge, Henrik watches with horror how an attack vessel is on a direct collision course with Joanna's Kylo ship. The drone supply is almost wiped out completely and the missiles from behind them just keep coming and coming. He moves over to the observation window and he sees how the Kylo ship fires projectiles and pulse beams frantically towards the incoming ship, but it's too late.

"Henrik to Joanna, come in!" he says over the com.

With despair in her voice, she answers.

"My love, this might be the end for me I have ordered the crew to get to safety inside the emergency pods. I will close the door to my pod now. My dear Henrik, rescue us!"

"I will my love!" he says, knowing that there is nothing more he can do right now, he can feel the salty taste on his tongue from a teardrop running down his cheek. With a bit of luck her pod will be able to get to a safe enough distance from *Kalypso* before the collision.

Within half a minute, the attack vessel rams straight into *Kalypso*. The carnage is absolute, the ships merge into each other as metal melts due to heat and friction. Henrik is paralyzed, his world goes dark, empty of space and time. *Kraken* has taken heavy damage, fire is spread throughout the ship. The crew is desperate and Henrik holds his breath.

Bjorn has isolated himself and is solely focused on the *Kraken*'s main weapon. He reports that it's fully charged, no answer. He decides to fire.

"Fire!" Bjorn shouts. No one hears it but the hull of the entire ship glows as the energy accumulates and within seconds is sent towards *Exitium*. A pulse blast like nothing ever witnessed fills the void between the two ships.

The energy from the blast demolishes Tidus' ship. What once was a huge battleship is now divided into huge chunks of scrap metal. The battle scene goes silent as Chronos' remaining vessel isn't sure about how to handle the sudden loss.

Within minutes, everything goes silent except from the remaining fires that continue to fill sections with smoke as the extinguisher systems are emptied.

Epilogue!

H enrik wakes up on the metal floor of the bridge. Dust and a smell of electrical fire fill his lungs. He isn't sure what happened, why he was unconscious. Bjorn picks him up on his feet. His ears are ringing but he's not sure why.

He opens his mouth.

"Joanna," is all he manages to say.

"We are looking for her. Her signature should soon be identified as we salvage all the escape pods out there. We won!" Bjorn says. He almost can't believe it himself as he still struggles to understand how they survived the battle.

"Help me to the command seat. I need to find her!" Henrik orders.

"Calm down, Commander, didn't you hear what I said? We are looking for her, we won, the battle is over, we are victorious, my friend," Bjorn says as he helps Henrik sit down in the seat.

The seat feels cold. He leans forwards, letting his

thigh support his elbows, pinching the spot on his nose between his brows with his thumb and index finger. He is tired and even the fact that they won the battle doesn't give him any satisfaction. He must find Joanna; it's the only thought in his mind.

"Bjorn, bring up the search party on the screen. How many confirmed pods do we have floating?" Henrik asks, pointing towards the screen in front of him. Bjorn does as he is told and within seconds, they follow the search and rescue team who just left *Kraken* on their way towards the pods.

The scene near where *Kalypso* used to be is filled with debris and darkened metal fused to each other. All smaller pieces of the ships are scattered as the impact pushed them away rapidly. All that is left now is an unrecognizable metal formation of what once was two vessels. As the search and rescue team nears the area, they find a lot of destroyed pods. The scene is horrific as the unforgiving coldness of space has taken a death grip upon those unfortunate enough to be hit by the debris.

Bjorn claps Henrik on his shoulder to reassure him that they will find her.

"The search and rescue will take a couple of hours minimum, but don't worry, the oxygen supply in each pod is enough for at least two days," Bjorn says.

Henrik takes a heavy breath. "I trust you, my friend, bring her home."

Directly after the battle, the Chronos attack vessel that was left alive moved away to an appropriate distance. The captain of the ship hailed Henrik on the communications and declared itself under his command. The mood on *Kraken* is a mixed feeling of great joy that the battle is won, and at the same time, they are drowning in sorrow as they remember the great loss the battle meant for them all.

Henrik activates the ship-wide intercom. It's time to speak to the crew.

"This is your commander speaking, I wish to thank you all for the effort and sacrifice you all have made in our journey towards victory. In this first battle, we are victorious." He takes a deep breath before continuing. "We were hit hard, and our losses will be felt and remembered for a very long time. Despite our losses we must not lose our spirit. We will mourn, and we will remember. The hardest and most difficult part is still ahead of us, but for now, let's take a moment of silence and give our lost friends and family members the respect and honour they deserve," he says. In silence, he clenches his fist and hopes that Joanna's pod soon will be found.

Shortly after the moment of silence, Henrik receives a private hail through the intercom. It's Evan's voice.

"Commander, I've analysed all events before and just after the destruction of *Exitium*. I've isolated a suspicious energy signature of a miniature hyperspace jump," he reports.

"Do you have more information, Evan?"

"Unfortunately, I can't say that I do, Commander. I'm running additional analyses of the signature as we speak," Evan says.

The End.

Final words

When Henrik previously got introduced by Evan regarding the way the ships work, he learnt that most of the time both the cannons and the missiles are fired automatically by the ships' AI.

He smiles as he remembers how Evan described it with such bluntness, still hearing his words as he described it.

"...their ability to react often exceeds the organic brain's abilities regarding timing and aiming, so it's both impractical and foolish to only have organics, pardon my roughness, in command, organics should only be able to choose primary targets, that's it."

Special Thank You!

I would like to direct my deepest gratitude for my special backers of this book project, thank you my dear mother **Ann-Cristin Vuolo Junros** and **Adrian Gibbons** for your support towards getting this book professionally edited and ready for publications.

As Ultimate Backers on the Kickstarter campaign I am forever grateful for your belief in me and the books potential.

And Adrian, I hope your dream of being published comes true one day, I want to be the first to place the pre-order and to have the chance to read your story.

Reviews wanted!

D ID YOU LIKE THE STORY IN THIS BOOK? IF SO, I WOULD GREATLY APPRECIATE YOUR HELP. Please leave a review. I would appreciate it tremendously if you would take a few minutes to leave a review- just a sentence or two stating that you liked the book is all it takes. Think of it as leaving a tip after a meal you've enjoyed. That will help make it possible for me to continue pursuing my love of writing. Fewer than 2% of readers leave reviews. Please be the exception. Thank you.

Make sure to check out the merch and NFT *(with utility and perks for owner)* available for purchase in our merch store. (Available in Q4 2022).

SITE   FACEBOOK   INSTAGRAM

About the Author

My name is Christoffer Vuolo Junros (1989), I was born and raised in Gothenburg, Sweden's second largest city. As I write this I live in Stockholm with my wonderful wife Joanna, she's an amazing person who captured my heart with love.

I consider myself a sci-fi nerd who enjoys writing, exploring cutting-edge technology, and immersing myself in a story, developing my characters based on their unique characteristics.

I work hard to achieve my goals and always have at least one project on going. One of my main interests in life is futuristic technology, thus I strive to be a pioneer or at least an early adopter of interesting technologies that comes my way, "technology" for me is a tool for us to make our lives easier, act as an extended arm with the aim of simplifying tasks and giving us new skills.

Beside writing I own and operate a small clothing company in addition to my day job as an engineer. As a senior design engineer, I've worked for companies such as Volvo, Scania, SAAB, and Husqvarna.

You can connect with me on:
- https://originandromeda.com
- https://twitter.com/originandromeda
- https://facebook.com/originandromeda
- https://junros.se

Made in the USA
Coppell, TX
27 December 2022

90689800R00184